FALCON GUARD

ROBERT WINTER

An Original Publication from Robert Winter Books

To request permission and all other inquiries, contact Robert Winter at robertwinterauthor@comcast.net or www.robertwinterauthor.com.

First Publication, April 2025

ISBN: 978-1-948883-20-7

Printed in the United States of America

For Peter, again, for all his love and support

MAP OF ICELAND

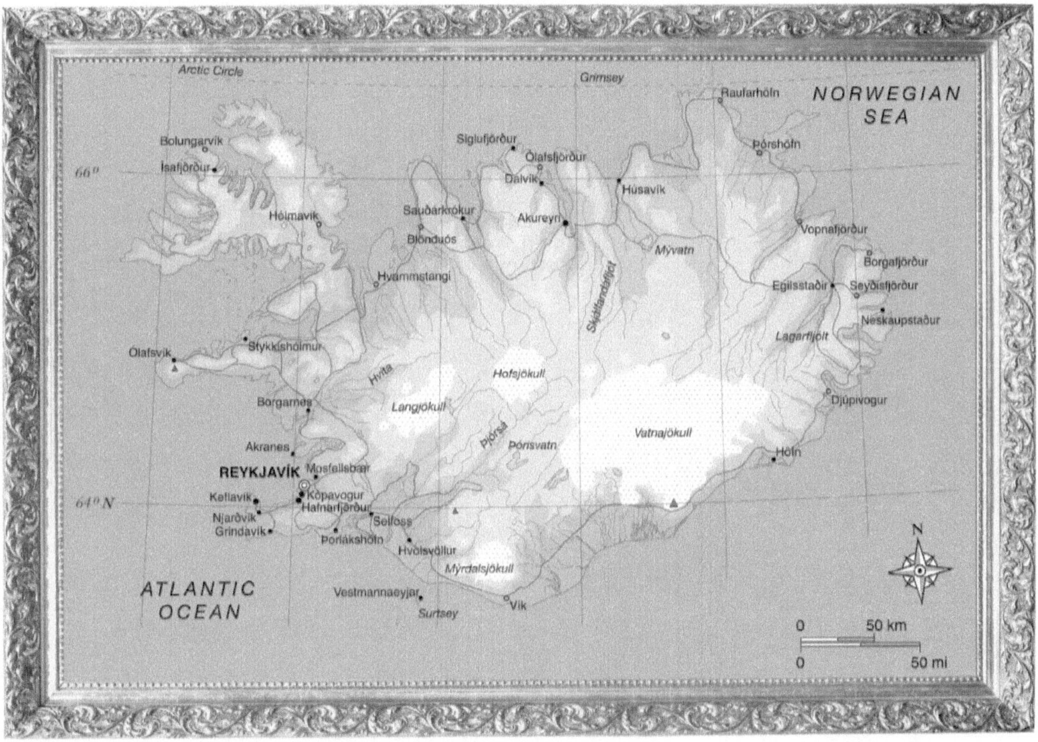

CHAPTER
ONE

Not thirty minutes after a ghoul cat had dealt a life-ending blow to Altair, Magnús stared after the miraculous human as Diwata took him to the nearby pond to clean off dried blood.

Altair had slept a bit after his inexplicable healing, Magnús keeping watch over him. When he woke, Ólafur pulled a shirt and pants from his pack for Altair to change into. Now the cousins tended to each other's wounds as best they could, watching Diwata and Altair walk away. Ólafur traced a glyph in the air over Magnús's ribs and invoked Eir, the goddess of healing. The ache eased, and Magnús began to breathe more easily.

Ólafur's mental voice carried amazement as he worked. «What in the name of Hel just happened?»

Magnús's mind rang with his own astonishment, and he could only shrug. He drew magic to power the glyph he sketched over Ólafur. «I have no idea. Something that heals itself from fatal wounds? I've never heard of such a being in Iceland.»

«Perhaps it's in the nature of Altair's magic rather than his parentage. Diwata and I have been discussing ways to get at the enchantment that controls or threatens him. Maybe when we solve that, Altair's nature will reveal itself.»

Magnús walked over to the body of the dead woman who had been a ghoul cat. She was smallish as a human, less than half the size of the beast she became. Blood pooled in the gravel under her.

"What did you shoot her with?" Ólafur asked aloud.

"Silver bullets," Magnús said. "Bryndís told me that a mirror will mesmerize an urðarköttur for a time, though we don't know how Altair guessed that. Only silver bullets can kill it. Bryndís had someone pack the gun in with our supplies, but it didn't occur to me the beast would find us so easily."

He grunted in frustration. "I should have been better prepared. Altair would have died if he wasn't...whatever he is."

"And the prophecy says if Altair dies, Iceland dies." Ólafur was silent a moment. "You're too hard on yourself, Cousin. You took every precaution, and when the attack came, we handled it. Altair was in the way, but that was bad luck, not a failing on your part."

Magnús didn't respond. He knew he'd failed. As he always suspected he would. For the hundredth time, he wondered why the Nornir engaged him in this prophecy. Altair was more than a pawn of fate. He was a gentle, sparkling young man who deserved a long and happy life. He needed someone stronger to keep him safe, someone with fewer failures on his balance sheet.

"You're thinking of Sigurjón, aren't you?" Ólafur asked. Magnús glared at him sharply until Ólafur held up both hands placatingly. "I didn't look into your mind. But I know that brooding look. It isn't hard to follow your thoughts from Altair to Sigurjón."

"Why do you say that?"

Ólafur cocked his head. "Surely you see it."

"Assume I don't."

"You were in love with a young human, and you felt like you

failed him. Now you feel like you're failing Altair. Since you have feelings for Altair, it's natural you'd be reminded of the past."

"I'm not in love with Altair," Magnús responded immediately. He couldn't be. They'd just met. Yes, Altair was handsome. He had wit and courage, a spark of life that was precious, an air of self-effacement combined with backbone...

"I'm not," Magnús insisted again, but more softly.

"Whatever you say, Cousin." Ólafur lightly punched his good shoulder. "It's been a century since you lost Sigurjón. There is no dishonor to his memory if you love another. Even in the best of circumstances, you will never have more than a mortal's lifespan to spend with any human. I can't believe someone worthy of your love would expect you to remain solitary after he dies."

Magnús snorted dismissively. "Anyway, Altair doesn't want to stay in Iceland. And don't forget the rest of that prophecy. What I may or may not want is irrelevant even if I succeed in whatever it is the Nornir expect of me."

"Your doom," Ólafur said gravely. "I know. But 'doom' is not the same thing as a death sentence."

Magnús could hear Altair and Diwata returning from the stream, talking softly. "No more, Óli. We can't talk about this around Altair without risking a seizure, and it doesn't matter anyway. Two days until the new moon. Less, really, since it's well after midnight. We need to sleep and get moving as soon as it's light."

When the humans joined them, Diwata grimaced at the corpse. "I can take care of that," she said, gesturing with her chin. "After Lady Bryndís told us about the urðarköttur, I studied them a bit. They come from a cat buried in a graveyard, subjected to sorcery, and left for three years. I don't think they can rise a second time, but I've got a counter spell that should help before we bury her. It."

"You two go rest," Ólafur said. "You need to be ready for Grýla. I'll keep watch the rest of the night with Diwata."

Magnús nodded wearily, then said, "That screaming noise. That was your spell, too?"

Diwata grinned. "It's from Óli's favorite metal band. I added it to your lightstones in case we didn't see the flashing. Pretty great, wasn't it?"

Altair groaned. "It was so loud I thought my ears would burst."

"Really?" Ólafur looked thoughtful. "The magic cry was intense, but I wouldn't say painfully so. Did either of you experience pain with it?" Both Magnús and Diwata murmured denials. "Perhaps your race is one with exceptional hearing. Another clue we can work with."

"It was sharp, like it was cutting into my brain." Altair stopped talking suddenly, his eyes narrowing in concentration. "Cut. Something about a blade..."

"What about a blade?" Magnús asked.

"When *this* happened"—Altair gestured down at his chest and belly—"I think I heard a voice. It said something about finding a blade."

"May I?" Ólafur gestured vaguely at Altair's head. "Perhaps I can help find the memory."

"Um, I'd rather Magnús try. No offense, Óli. It's just...he's already been in there a lot."

Magnús tried to conceal the rush of pleasure in his gut. Altair trusted him still, even though Magnús's mistake about the urðarköttur should have killed him.

Although it wasn't necessary for mental contact, he rested his hand on Altair's shoulder and reached out gently with his huldufólk gifts. Altair's mind was so familiar to him already. Magnús skimmed the surface of it like a skater on a frozen pond, trying not to go too deeply, though he selfishly wanted to know

Altair's private thoughts. He revisited recent memories—Altair and Diwata talking about magical energies and theories on how it worked, Altair shivering in the cold water as he cleaned blood from his body and wondered if Magnús would think he was too skinny—

Stop that, Altair said in his mind, chidingly. *Too personal.*

—Altair looking at the body of the person that was supposed to have been his mentor, Altair watching his wounds heal and hearing a voice in his head, the words so soft and vague he couldn't really remember, but yes, something about using the blade to "know himself."

The memory was gone. Magnús disengaged their thoughts respectfully but couldn't resist stroking Altair's hair before withdrawing his hand.

When he related the memory he'd found, Diwata chewed her lower lip thoughtfully. "A blade to help Altair know himself. It isn't reminding me of any spell I know, but I'll think about it."

"Perhaps Lady Bryndís will have some idea," Ólafur suggested.

The two wandered off, softly discussing how to proceed. Magnús leaned in and said quietly in Altair's ear, "You are not too skinny."

INTERLUDE

Sigurjón finished herding his flock into their enclosure, biting back his impatience at the most stubborn ram, Loki. His mother called to him from the open front door to the house. Obsessed with impressing the pastor with how smart her children were, Mamma no doubt wanted him to work on his catechism with his younger brothers and little sister.

He pretended not to hear her. Instead, he hurried away from the red-roofed house, uphill to the where the moss gave way to the stony base of the hill that sheltered their farm. Sigurjón vowed silently he would spend an hour later with the children to help them. Alda was quick as a whip; she'd be fine. But Eðvarð struggled, and their pabbi was prone to beating lessons into his sons. Yes, Eðvarð would get Sigurjón's full attention. Later.

Because now, he was at the edge of the crevasse that led deep into the hill. He followed the runoff from the hot spring, making his way farther up the fissure, until the way opened to a flat area at the bottom of a shaft of stone.

Looking up the stony walls to the opening at the top, to the blue sky visible above him, he smiled. The warmth of the hot spring was trapped here delightfully, and the moss was green as the emeralds he'd seen in a book. With any luck, *he* would be somewhere nearby—

"Sigurjón."

The deep, melodious voice echoing in the chamber from out of the empty air had a teasing edge to it. Sigurjón laughed as if he were as young as Alda. Hands outstretched, he hurried from rock to rock that protruded from the spring, grasping at empty air, following little chuckles.

"Magnús, stop teasing me," he protested when his arms remained empty.

"As you wish."

Suddenly, Magnús appeared right in front of him. His fine, silver-blond hair was tied in a tail, and his blue eyes sparkled. Sigurjón stepped happily into his embrace. He was fully a head shorter than Magnús, Sigurjón's...what? His huldumaður? His friend? Lover?

Words didn't matter. The way Magnús kissed him felt so much better than when Gréta Þórisdóttir had cornered him outside of her father's barn.

"You smell of sheep," Magnús teased him between kisses. "I never thought I'd grow to like the smell so much."

Sigurjón chuckled. "If I stink, then let's go to that pool you showed me before. When I'm naked and helpless, you can work your huldufólk magic and lure me away to your underground kingdom."

Magnús threw back his head and laughed. "My 'underground kingdom,' as you call it, smells of sheep as well, thanks to my cousin Ólafur. He's taken to reading texts on livestock breeding that he borrows invisibly from the library at that school that opened recently in Reykjavik."

"The University of Iceland? I'd like to attend there." Sigurjón entwined his fingers with Magnús's as the elf led him deeper into the fissure toward the chamber where the spring filled a natural basin, creating a hot pot.

"Really? What would you like to study?"

"Oh, so many things." Sigurjón blew out his breath in a whoosh. "It's such an exciting time. With the Great War over, things are changing. I've heard men talking after church. Money is coming to Iceland from other countries. Pabbi got the best price ever for our lambs this spring. People are saying there will be roads, maybe a railroad to move people around."

"My human dreamer," Magnús said fondly. "This country has a long memory. I'm not sure it would tolerate being weighed down with train tracks by the race that brought sheep to eat all its forests."

They reached the chamber with the pool. Light filtered down from an opening above, through which Sigurjón could see a patch of blue. The waft of sulfur in the air, the breath of warm steam drifting to them, made him itch to be submerged in water, entangled with his huldumaður. They stripped and gingerly entered the warm water, careful not to slip on the rocks.

Magnús sighed lustily as he settled into the pool. It was a little too hot for Sigurjón at first; sometimes that was a bad sign, when the heat of the waters rose. The country had a temper and tended to show its frustration in violent fits and starts.

Seeing Sigurjón's discomfort, Magnús took his hand and whispered a few words in that strange tongue of his. His eyes flashed from an icy blue almost to white, and then Sigurjón sighed in relief as the pool went from near-scalding to pleasantly hot. He sank down next to Magnús, their bare skin connecting. Magnús's arm came around his shoulders, the warm water stirred his excitement...

Afterwards, they spread their clothes and stretched out on a rocky ledge that bordered the pool. The bright blue sky visible through the crack in the roof of the cavern told Sigurjón he had plenty of time before he'd really be missed.

Magnús stirred and reached for his clothes. From the pouch he always carried, he withdrew a clump of gray weeds with blue flowers. "I found this draumagras growing in the shelter of a tall willow." He grinned playfully. "Would you like to dream of the future?"

"Of course I would," Sigurjón exclaimed. "So much is changing, I want to see where it's all heading."

"Very well." Magnús leaned over and began weaving the stems of draumagras into Sigurjón's unruly hair. When he finished, he kissed Sigurjón, then said, "Lie back. Close your eyes and rest. I'll keep watch and make sure you don't sleep too long."

Sigurjón smiled up at him. "I trust you."

"Think on what you want to know or to see as you fall asleep."

That was easy—Sigurjón wanted to know what was in store for Iceland. He made himself more comfortable and closed his eyes as Magnús began to sing a soft melody. It was not anything like the music Sigurjón knew, and its words were in that strange tongue Magnús spoke sometime. The language of the huldufólk. The song crept into the corners of Sigurjón's head, loosening his limbs even more than the warm water, easing his small aches from a day in the field with the sheep, carrying him...away.

In his dream, he opened his eyes and found himself alone. He seemed to be on his family's farm, yet the outbuilding he thought he recognized faded away as he watched. Other buildings of some kind took its place, spreading over the land. These structures were huge in scale, much larger even than the storage silos he saw when he helped his father bring the sheep to market.

And people. So many people! The colors and textures of their clothing were unlike anything he'd even seen in life. Men and women, they moved quickly, with purpose, along paths that wove among the strange buildings. He heard Icelandic speech but mixed with words and phrases every bit as strange as Magnús's tongue: "banking crisis," "online," "social media," "airport."

And where was Magnús in this exciting new world? As Sigurjón thought of his lover, the scene changed. He didn't know where he was, but the rocky cliff, the field dotted with hummocks, the dark sea just beginning to turn gold as it caught the dawn... It all felt like Iceland. He saw only one building, painted in oddly garish colors. It reminded him of the lighthouse he'd seen once.

Moving as one could only in a dream, Sigurjón rose up into the sky to see better where he was. On the beach below, people were milling about. Dressed even more strangely than the first people he'd spied, many of those on the shore seemed to be wearing tight black clothes that covered their bodies. The people were pulling crafts onto the strand. But these weren't like the wooden boats Sigurjón knew. These were sleek and large, mostly painted white, and made from some material he didn't recognize.

It all brought a tinge of fear to the sleeper. What was happening? Who were these people? Uneasy, he looked around. Was Magnús here?

And then Sigurjón gasped as he saw him, standing on the edge of a cliff, arms spread wide. Magnús in this vision looked more stern and fearsome than Sigurjón had ever seen. He looked...well, not older, but much harder than the huldumaður Sigurjón knew.

This Magnús glowed from within, light burning under his skin and shining out of his eyes. His clothes were torn, he was dirtied, and he seemed to have been fighting. In one hand, he grasped a dagger made of silver fire. A falcon was perched on his other arm, its wings spread as it called out its defiance in a ringing note that Sigurjón felt in his soul. They were fighting the strangely garbed men and women on the beach. And they were... They were...

Sigurjón paused, unable to put a name to the strange feelings that made his heart leap, tightened his gut, and sent shivers down his dream-fuddled arms.

Magnificent. That was the word. Huldumaður and falcon, guarding Iceland. Pride in Magnús swelled in Sigurjón's chest. He wanted to cheer and to weep at the same time, though he had no idea why.

"My love? Sigurjón, wake up."

Magnús's voice confused Sigurjón, because the huldumaður standing defiant with the falcon on his arm was not speaking. Then a hand shook his shoulder gently, and he opened his eyes. Magnús, again soft and kind, looked down at him, concern on his face.

"You began to cry, my love. Was it something you glimpsed?"

Sigurjón shook his head uncertainly, but trails of wetness dampened his cheeks. Already the dream was confused. Fading. "You were...I don't know. With a falcon. And, and...a knife?"

Magnús ran a hand through Sigurjón's hair, soothing him and gently untangling the draumagras. "Did you dream of the future?"

"I...I think I did. It was so..." Sigurjón didn't know how to describe anything he remembered. He lacked the words, and the images were slipping from his grasp.

"We should get you back," Magnús said, after Sigurjón had been silent for several moments. "You'll be missed."

They rose and dressed again. In silence, they walked hand in hand back along the rocks and through the fissure. When they emerged from the shelter of the hill and Sigurjón's home was in sight below, Magnús stopped. He lowered his head to kiss Sigurjón one more time.

"Again next week?" he asked.

Sigurjón nodded. Still in the fading grip of the draumagras dream, though, he suddenly shuddered. He felt a terrible presentiment that he would not meet Magnús again for a very, very long time.

"No. I will see you again," Sigurjón said fiercely, though he didn't quite know why. Surprise showed in the huldumaður's eyes. "I love you, Magnús."

And Sigurjón turned away reluctantly, to hurry home.

CHAPTER

THREE

A few hours after Altair's recovery, the troupe carefully crossed the Dimmuborgir lava field. Altair stumbled slightly where rocky soil mixed with bits of pumice.

A fog had risen, obscuring the sun, though not yet so heavy as to blind them to their surroundings. The scrub trees were far from lovely, but it was the twisted fingers of basalt pointing at the sky, black and menacing, that made Altair shiver. In places, domes of volcanic rock jutted up, revealing deep crevasses or openings to caves.

What was in those, Altair wondered, hiding in the dark? The fog added an aura of gloom that he did not like at all. The satchel on his shoulder felt awkward and heavy; he wished he'd left it behind in case he suddenly had to run, although even the thought of leaving it made him uncomfortable.

"This landscape looks like it was boiled," he muttered.

"More or less correct," Ólafur said. "I believe the lava that erupted here passed over a lake, which created lots of steam. The steam caused the lava to bubble or move in different ways while also causing it to cool rapidly. Hence...." He gestured widely at the menacing shapes that loomed ahead.

"It reminds me of a medieval castle," Diwata said from ahead of Altair. "Or maybe like the hand of a giant, reaching up through the ground to grab us."

"Don't," Altair said, shuddering. It was far too easy to imagine just that, a monstrous hand with an excess of digits waiting until the group was in its palm, then breaking through the crust of the earth to capture them and squeeze.

Although the true location of the troll they sought was apparently hidden, Magnús's talent had narrowed down the possibilities to this bizarre nightmare of a landscape. When they'd arrived at the parking area for a company that ran tours of the site, though, he confessed with some consternation that he couldn't get them any closer. So Diwata had pulled the borrowed wayfinder stone, wrapped in silk, from her pouch.

Now as they followed Diwata, Magnús was on alert already. Altair had grown to recognize the elf's stance, poised and ready to move into action if needed. One hand hovered near his belt pouch, close to the enchanted stones he deployed. Magnús had made a few more before they left their campsite.

The faded marks on Altair's chest still itched at the memory of Magnús shooting the werecat. He recalled Magnús standing over his bound body just yesterday morning back at the university, fighting off Sigmundsdóttir. Now she was dead and Altair was not, though he should be. His feet stumbled and his stomach lurched with nausea. Too much. It was all just...too much.

"Y-you said trolls turn to stone in daylight," he muttered to Magnús. "Does that work even with this fog? I can barely tell where the sun is."

Magnús looked grim. "It...should still turn them. But I can't say I've tested the theory."

A rumble through the ground, the groan of forces beneath the surface, brought the party to a halt. *Maybe it's not just my nerves.*

Magnús crouched and looked around rapidly, as if preparing for an assault. Altair's gaze flew from cave opening to crevasse to black columns of basalt. If this was an attack, where would it come from? There were so many dark openings and shadowed breaks...

The rumble subsided quickly, and Magnús straightened again. "Just another tremor then. This area is highly volcanic still, though I don't recall hearing of a significant eruption in centuries."

That should have made Altair feel better, but instead it keyed him up further. He'd grown to respect the raw power of this country, the churning lava, vents that were far too awake. All of nature's restrained fury ready to remind fragile mortals and elves, too, that they were merely ants crawling across the surface of a not-quite-slumbering behemoth.

Movement from the corner of his eye made Altair's head whirl round. He peered intently, eyes narrowed. Black, crooked fingers of basalt stretched toward the sky. The fog was growing thicker, more gray, but still he could see oddly well in every direction. He kept scanning the columns, trying to identify where the motion had come from.

One lava pillar caught his attention. Irregular and jagged as the others, yet toward the top it became smoother, almost mounded. Funny. At the very top there were two little points like ears. And down the side of the column was a blacker streak, thick, curling around the lava like a vine.

The vine moved.

Altair's yelp had Magnús at his side in an instant. "What did you see?" the elf demanded. Following Altair's pointing finger, Magnús peered into the fog. "How can you see...? Wait! There. I think our approach has been spotted."

The fog swirled slightly, lightening the area a bit. Diwata

inhaled sharply, then said in a hoarse whisper, "No freakin' way! It's just a folktale, I thought."

Ólafur joined them on Altair's other side. "Is that...?"

Magnús nodded, then called out, "Hail, Jólaköttur. We mean no harm but ask to speak with thy mistress."

Altair had to stifle another yelp as the black shape stirred and lifted its head. Two glowing orange eyes opened wide in the black face. The vine twitched again and now Altair realized it was a thick and furry tail. Silhouetted against the foggy sky, the head bent to lick at a raised paw, and suddenly Altair got it.

"A cat!" he hissed softly. "Is it another urðarköttur like the professor?"

Diwata muttered, "Worse if the legends are true."

The cat on the column fixed its orange eyes on Altair and paused in cleaning its enormous foreleg.

"I am myself alone," it said in a rumbling voice that put Altair in mind of the menacing tones of a tiger he'd heard once in a zoo.

It rose then, black and towering on top of the column, stretched, and leapt lightly to the ground. The size of a pony, it casually made its way toward them, stepping gingerly, almost distastefully, over the rocky ground. But it never took its glowing eyes off Altair.

Magnús moved between Altair and the advancing cat creature, reaching for the stones in his belt pouch. The cat tracked the movement and pricked its ears forward and up. White, needle-sharp teeth appeared in what Altair had to call a smile.

"Peace, elf," the cat purred. "It is not yet my season for hunting the wicked and the lazy. Your human child there is not yet ready for Grýla's pot."

Magnús lowered his hand to his side, away from his belt. "Indeed, it is many months still until Yuletide."

"Yet the fire under Grýla's pot never goes out." The cat paused ten feet away from the group and sat gracefully on its haunches, thick tail coiling around its forelegs. "The stew she makes is a rich affair, though the meat is at first tough and stringy. Carefully she tends to it, tasting the broth, adjusting the mix. Perhaps a bit more of that naughty child in the larder will add to the depth of flavor."

Its eyes moved to look over Altair's shoulder. "Or an exotic ingredient, for novelty. Diwata Naómi Pétursdóttir. I remember you well. There was a year of rebellion, of not tending to your chores properly. You did not receive a gift of clothes that year. I crept through your window and sat at the foot of your bed, considering whether to take you."

A rattling noise came out of the evil-looking mouth, and Altair realized it was a laugh. "But your mother's ways were not of the Yule and so I granted you another year. Fortunately for you, some discipline returned to your life, and the next December, new clothes were piled on the foot of your bed. I passed you by."

Diwata's breath had grown shaky. "Th-thank you, Yule Cat."

"But you." The glowing eyes fixed on Altair again. "I have not wandered a nighttime street on which you slept. Yet you are of this land. How is this?"

Magnús said, "He is newly arrived in this country from America, night-stalking Jólaköttur. Some of his people came from Iceland. Perhaps it is their flavor you scent."

"Hrrrm, possibly," the Yule Cat granted. "But no matter. My mistress would find his meat makes her stew foul." The laughing rustle returned.

Altair wondered what the joke was; before he could ask, the cat stood and turned.

"Grýla will speak with you." It moved forward into the fog without looking to see if the group followed. But of course, they did.

The mist had grown thicker again. Though the Yule Cat was only a few yards ahead of them, already it was harder to make out as it wove among the lava pillars.

"I can't see anything," Diwata said.

Altair put a hand to her elbow to guide her forward after the cat. Tail lashing, it led them to a large, wide structure, a thick bubble of hardened lava with a black maw that made Altair think uncomfortably of a mouth.

So of course the Yule Cat walked straight into it and disappeared in the darkness.

The group paused for a moment, but Ólafur sighed. "Nothing for it but to enter, I suppose."

"When we meet Grýla, be extremely respectful," Magnús said. "Her temper is legendary. I expect the Yule Lads should be idle at this time of year, but they will come rapidly if she calls."

"Yule Lads?" Altair mumbled. "That doesn't sound so bad."

Diwata gave a nervous laugh. "Thirteen trolls with names like Meat Hook and Door Slammer. Hard pass on meeting them."

Magnús led the way into the mouth of the lava cave, Altair right behind. It was pitch-black inside, and he heard Ólafur curse as he stumbled over something. Magnús pulled a stone out of his pouch and muttered a few words. The blue glow changed to a gentle yellow light that grew until Altair could see better.

They were inside a largish cavern that sloped down toward the back. A swish of tail, only just blacker than the gloom, showed them the way the Yule Cat had gone, so the party followed carefully. The rough path was wide, strewn with broken and fallen pieces of lava. The glow from Magnús's stone didn't reach the roof, but on the walls, Altair could see patches of fantastic color: oranges and yellows and blues.

"That must be oxidation from minerals in the lava," he said, excited despite himself. "The formation is very different from the few caves I've explored in the States. No stalactites here. And look! The walls are striated. You can see where the lava—"

"Later," Magnús whispered back and gestured ahead where a flickering glow had appeared around a turning. "We're there."

CHAPTER

FOUR

Altair followed the others into an enormous cavern, so vast the walls quickly spread beyond the glow of Magnús's stone. Broken bits of crates and furniture, heaps of discarded cloth, and other junk lay scattered about the floor. The air smelled of wood smoke, barely masking some stench Altair couldn't identify but that turned his stomach.

A fire crackled in the center of the cavern. On the pile of logs was a huge black kettle, rough-made, easily large enough to hold two or three grown men. And stirring the kettle with a plank at least four feet long was a hideous mound of troll.

At least Altair assumed it was a troll, based on the description the others had given him. Its skin seemed made from chunks of gray rock, and it stood more than twice as tall as any human. Magnús had mentioned the name 'Grýla Trollmother', and chest-high lumps suggested breasts. Altair gathered this troll was female; without those clues, he couldn't have guessed a gender.

Stringy black hair hung down where she bent her head over the kettle, obscuring her face. Some rags were wrapped around her body in semblance of clothes. Her legs were bent into a bow-

21

legged crouch, and the hands that gripped the paddle were the size of hubcaps, ending in sharp shale-like fragments.

Her head rose from the kettle as she turned to stare at the party. Large eyes, bright green and surprisingly human-looking in that craggy face, passed over each in turn. Then they came back to rest on Altair.

Without releasing his gaze, and with a deliberate movement, the troll stretched a hand to a crate near the fire, pulled out a hunk of meat that resembled—*Nope, not thinking about it. No, no, no*—and tossed it into the pot. The splash that followed kicked up drops of a thick liquid.

The Yule Cat strolled into the circle of firelight, sat, and gazed up at the troll. "Grýla Child's Bane, these are the intruders. Two of the huldufólk, a human bred of two lands, and one that looks human but is far from."

Grýla released the paddle so it sank slightly into her stew. She rose up on thick legs that reminded Altair of the lava columns in the plain above.

"Huldufólk, have you brought these children here for my pot?" Her voice was crumbly somehow, like the sound rocks make when rubbed together.

Magnús stepped forward and made a bow. "Grýla Troll-mother, we come at the advice of my cousin, seeking knowledge only you possess."

Grýla grunted. "I wonder if that silver tongue would enjoy a taste of my stew." Altair heard Magnús swallow hard at the thought. But Grýla turned and shuffled toward a cabinet standing on the floor. She opened it and rummaged around, emerging with a few large vegetables. All the while, Altair had the sense her attention remained on the group, specifically on him.

"We have come seeking wisdom only the Trollmother possesses," Magnús continued. "Knowledge of why the trolls are snatching humans near the cities."

Grýla snorted. "Ask the Mountain King. Long centuries have nurtured his discontent until even he listens to bad counsel from one who claims kinship."

The last word was accompanied by a glare right at Ólafur. The Trollmother picked up her paddle again and returned to her stew.

"Kinship," Magnús said, understanding in his voice. "You know who Ólafur's brother is."

"Trouble that one is," the Yule Cat said as it groomed itself, a shockingly pink tongue bathing a raised paw that it then swiped over its ear. "But far from lazy, oh yes. Very industrious, in fact, since returning to this land."

Ólafur groaned. "What is Lars up to now?"

Grýla grimaced as she stirred more forcefully. "Another elf with a silver tongue. Making things shiny and bright, promising the Night Trolls that the day could again be theirs. My poor stupid kin forget that even before Man, the day was their enemy. But though they eat of Grýla's pot, they ignore Grýla's warnings."

"The queen should have listened to me," Magnús growled through gritted teeth, his anger palpable. "Lars is uniting the trolls in some scheme against the humans, isn't he? That's why they have been acting strangely."

"Trolls and other of the night folk," the Yule Cat said lazily as he continued his cleaning. "Some think to harness a troll's power but forget the greed and willfulness that go with his strength. Grýla's folk hate the humans and yet long for their flesh. Dumb as oxen they may be, yet dangerous as bulls if they break their harness."

Grýla aimed a kick at the Yule Cat that it dodged easily though bestowing a baleful eye on his mistress. "Those are my children you mock," she grumbled.

"Fierce Grýla, will you share how Lars has gained the aid of the trolls?" Diwata asked.

The monstrous cook reached into a bag at her waist and

pulled out bits of root. She tossed them into the pot whose contents flared with sickly light. The shadows created on her face were terrible as she looked not at Diwata but at Altair.

"Before the ice, before the flood, this land belonged only to the trolls and the wights. Our strength is the strength of mountain and bedrock. Then came elf, dwarf, giant, godling. All were strangers to Miðgarður, all invaders from other realms. Their magics were different, we could not drive them out, and we could not eat them. So we learned to live with them. Then the meddling gods, for their own reasons, brought Man here, with his horses and his sheep and his crude instruments to rip up the ground." She laughed and bared her teeth. "We ate some of his brood and his livestock, but still Man came. My pot was never empty. It was a time of happiness."

"Not for the humans," Altair muttered.

"The Mountain King-that-was...was an idiot. He decided that the Æsir had brought Man for trolls to feast upon and so, when Man-villages grew too populous, he roused our people to cull them. The other races joined cause with Man, killed the Mountain King and thousands of my kin, and forced us back into the depths.

"And so we have lived for seven hundred years. Until one spawn of an invader race comes to the new Mountain King and whispers to him. Help him open a door, he says, and through it will come a new era for the trolls, back to the days before Man.

"The Mountain King believes him. Another idiot," she spat. "My kin believe him. Only Grýla does not believe in the door. And then what happens? Huldufólk arrive, bringing with them the key to the door-that-is-not."

"The key? Do you mean Alt—um, this human?" Magnús asked, gesturing at Altair.

"Doors are tricky things," she continued, apparently ignoring Magnús. "An invention of Man, a false hope of protection and privacy." She winked at her cat. "Useless against some, though. Eh, Jólaköttur?"

"Mrrrow," was the coy answer.

"Closed and locked, they may keep secrets forgotten for a troll's lifetime," Grýla continued. "Opened gently, some whispers leak out into the wind. But once smashed..." She shook her head. "The illusion is swept away, along with the door, the wall, the house, and the man who built it."

Magnús frowned. "Is there a house we need to find then?"

"Oh, for love of the gods," Diwata exclaimed and pushed at the elf's shoulder. "She isn't talking about a real door. Gah!" Bowing to Grýla, she said, "Fearsome Trollmother, if Altair is the key, then the door must be a magic ward of some kind. Presumably the way to use the key is sorcerous, which suggests... Witches?"

"No shirking here," the Yule Cat murmured, licking its raised paw.

"Witch, sorcerer, priest. Humans have too many labels for what is the same thing," Grýla complained, rummaging once more in her cabinet. The thing she pulled out was a greenish head of cabbage (Altair hoped) that she examined before throwing it into the kettle.

"Priest," Ólafur muttered in Magnús's ear. "It keeps coming back to that, doesn't it?"

Altair found he couldn't look away from the stewpot. The mixture simmering away with its odd mélange of vegetables and— he swallowed hard. Maybe it was a joke. Maybe Grýla and the Yule Cat were throwing in other kinds of creatures like a fox, or...well, what other kinds of animals did they have in Iceland?

Then Grýla's words came back to him. Something that could sweep away the man who built the house...

"If all the men are gone, what will you use in your pot?" The words came out of Altair in a rush before he could remember to be polite and respectful.

The Yule Cat growled at him, orange eyes narrowed, black tail lashing the air.

Grýla bared her teeth, chipped and shattered like shale. "My sons, my good-for-nothing husband, my kin, my kind. All would go hungry without Grýla's stew. All would suffer and complain about the weak broth, the lack of chunks of delicious meat. But do they see that? No!"

"So...you don't want the door to open?" Altair hazarded.

"This is why Vörður sent us to you," Magnús said firmly. "Something is building and you don't like it."

"Do you know about the"—Diwata darted a worried glance at Altair that he didn't understand, then said slowly to Grýla—"Black Priest?"

Something trembled inside Altair at that phrase. He had a brief burning sensation around his throat, similar to what he had experienced back in Hamarinn when he'd volunteered as a kind of Geiger counter. But this time the force or spell or whatever it was...it seemed weaker to Altair.

The Yule Cat rose, then stretched out its forelegs, arching its long back. To Diwata, it replied simply, "Do *you* know about the Black Priest? If not, there is work to be done lest I come throw you in my bag this Yuletide."

Altair felt Ólafur bristle next to him. "Don't threaten her. We're trying to understand, and I think you want to help us."

"Mind your tongue, elf," Grýla snapped. "Or I will rip it from your head and add some bitter-tasting álfur to the broth."

Ólafur opened his mouth to say more, but Diwata put a hand on his shoulder. "Can you tell us where to find the door?" she asked. "Or at least point us in the right direction? We want to stop this plan, too, and we believe time is running out. Like, in a matter of days."

Grýla shook her head, black hair hanging limp and straggly in the steam rising from her pot. "My children, my husband, even the Mountain King. Idiots they may be if they ignore her words, but still Grýla will not work against them."

"The land itself is warning of destruction in fire and flood, quake and storm," the Yule Cat said. "So *I* will heed the omens if my mistress will not, and offer as much aid as my contrary nature allows."

It leapt to the top of a tall, splintered cabinet, out of reach of the Trollmother. "I prowl the nighttime streets and hear whispers, sometimes of truth, sometimes of fear. And I am left wondering, how and where comes one of the huldufólk to be consecrated a priest, Black or otherwise? Who consecrated him? And to which god does he pay homage? Apply thy industry and, by the dark kind I serve and I rule, something better than a gift of clothing awaits thee."

CHAPTER

FIVE

Grýla turned her head abruptly toward the darkness opposite the way Magnús and the others had come in. A moment later, they heard echoes of rough laughter like rocks bouncing downhill in a landslide.

Jólaköttur sat on his perch and drew his tail around his legs. "Will you stay and meet some of my mistress's offspring? The Noisy Lads are playful." He rustled a dry laugh at them, orange eyes wide.

"Mother, do I smell fresh meat?" a voice boomed from the darkness.

"Did you send Jólaköttur to gather fresh supplies?" another asked.

"Brothers, perhaps our mother finally understands that the old ways are returning," added a third, chortling and very close now.

Grýla seemed tense as she returned to stirring her stewpot but made no comment. With a gesture, Magnús began to herd Altair, Diwata, and Ólafur out of the cavern, back the way they had come. He and Ólafur made themselves invisible as well as Altair

29

and Diwata. The Yule Cat tracked their movements across the cavern floor and to the passage but remained on his perch, grinning.

They stumbled hurriedly through the dark tunnels for a few yards until they made a turn and the light of Grýla's cave disappeared. Magnús risked one of his glowing stones and led the way up and into the open. Only then did he dare slow.

"We should be safe now under the sun," he murmured as he and Ólafur dropped their invisibility.

Altair was pale, and Diwata looked shaken. They shivered in the damp fog that surrounded them. The group was quiet as Magnús led the way back across the lava field and to the parked camper van.

"That was creepy shit," Altair muttered when they stood beside the camper once more. "What is with these demon cats in Iceland?"

"Careful," Ólafur said in a whisper. "Do nothing to irritate the Yule Cat. He might be out there; sunlight doesn't bother him."

"What do you think it was hinting at?" Diwata asked, rubbing her hands together for warmth.

Magnús shot an anxious glance at Altair, who threw his hands up in the air. "Fine, I get it. You can't talk about it in front of me. I'll go sit on that rock over there and hope I don't get eaten by an enchanted tabby."

"More likely to find a moðormur out there," Diwata said, adding an evil grin. "Don't worry, it's not a cat. More of a dog crossed with a worm that—"

"Stop teasing him," Magnús interrupted with a scowl for the witch. "Altair, don't go too far. We'll keep an eye on you."

When Altair was out of earshot but situated where Magnús could reach him quickly if needed, he turned back to Diwata and

Ólafur. "I think I heard the Yule Cat confirm that Lars is the Black Priest."

Ólafur looked pained. "It makes sense. When he returned from exile, Lars was different. More angry about humans than ever, hinting he'd find a way to solve all the problems they create in Iceland. He stopped honoring the Æsir entirely. One time, I saw him standing in Reykjavik in front of Hallgrímskirkja, laughing at the tourists and working little tricks to make them slip or to jam a door. It didn't seem like álfar magic, but I never pressed."

"Why did you not tell me this?" Magnús demanded.

Ólafur sighed. "Your anger with my brother makes you... unreasonable where he is concerned. I didn't want to distract you, and I doubted it was important. But it now seems likely Lars is at the heart of whatever is happening."

"So are you thinking this is like the story of Sæmundur?" Diwata asked. "He left Iceland and somehow found the Black School?"

Ólafur bent to pick up a loose piece of basalt, then flung it into the distance. "I'm not suggesting that it's the same as in the stories. But Lars wandered Miðgarður for many decades bent on his own prejudice and, probably, revenge on you, Magnús. Without access to his own magic, he could have remembered the stories of Icelanders who learned sorcery at the Black School. Perhaps he sought it out."

Magnús growled. "Queen Hildur should have listened to me."

Ólafur flushed and stepped closer to Magnús. "That's my brother you're talking about. I know you want him dead. *Everyone* knows that because you never stop talking about it. But even if we're right, maybe it's your fault Lars was out in the world in the first place."

"You blame me for wanting Lars punished? After what he did?"

"Simmer down, guys." Diwata put a hand on each of

Magnús's and Ólafur's clenched fists. "We need to get out of here and follow the Yule Cat's lead."

Ólafur looked sour at that but nodded. Magnús controlled his temper, too, though his pulse throbbed.

Diwata said, "There've been a lot of priests in Iceland who used black magic. Gottskálk the cruel. Galdra-Loftur."

"That name rings a bell," Magnús said, closing his eyes in concentration. "But I don't know where I've heard it."

"Plenty of bad stories about that dude," Diwata said. "Like, he practiced a spell by forcing a maid at his school in Hólar to iron her hands. Then he put a magic bridle on her and flew her through the air to visit his home. She had to be institutionalized after that. He killed another maid, can't remember why."

She paused. "Gottskálk was also tied to Hólar, remember? He was the big bad who wrote the Rauðskinna, the really wicked grimoire of magic. Galdra-Loftur supposedly memorized the Gráskinna, the gray book of magic, which was, like, medium strength evil. He wanted Gottskalk's red book so he could level up, I guess. It was all a long time ago. Gottskálk lived in the fifteen hundreds, I think, and Galdra-Loftur was around the seventeen hundreds."

"Still, two black magicians tied to Hólar, one a bishop who conceivably had a spell that creates a shackle of some kind..." Magnús shrugged. "The links to the prophecy are compelling. Also, Vörður was in Hólar for some reason when I stopped him, and he seems to know something of what Lars is up to. Whatever god Lars worships now, it makes sense it could be the same one Gottskálk and Galdra-Loftur followed."

Ólafur said, "Maybe the Yule Cat was telling us there is still a, what? A *cult* that lured Lars in."

"Lured. Lars wouldn't need much encouragement to work for the harm of humans." Magnús ignored the baleful look Ólafur gave him. "Anyway, I think we have to go to Hólar and investigate. We can start with the school you mentioned."

CHAPTER

SIX

L oftur Þorsteinsson emerged from the underground tunnel that connected the bishop's residence to his Latin school in Hólar. He should have been in class already, but he'd wanted to try the new galdur he'd developed. The only place to do that safely was in the hidden chamber below the residence, where the true scholars of this gods-forsaken place met in secret to share the dabs of arcane knowledge they amassed. None of them realized that Loftur, though still younger than most of them, was already the far superior magician.

Back in the school building, he hurried toward the classroom until a serving girl called to him quietly but urgently. She lurked in an alcove, half of her body in shadow.

Quickly checking that no one of importance was close, Loftur sauntered over. He had already studied the Grayskin Book of Sorcery thoroughly. In its pages he had learned many tricks to entrance women and make them compliant. The serving girls of his school made excellent subjects on which to practice, and he did so frequently and imaginatively.

"My sweet Helga. You want more of what I gave you last week, with the candle flames dancing on your breast?"

Helga shook her head nervously. "Loftur, my love, I am with child. *Your* child. I have kept it secret as long as I could, but soon someone will be able to tell."

"Ah." This was an inconvenience. After the experiment in which he bewitched a girl and rode her through the air like a little horse to visit a magician in Hólmavik, the bishop had threatened expulsion.

True, Loftur already had made his way through most of the grimoires the school possessed, but his search for the infamous Redskin Book was so far stymied. He couldn't leave the school until he'd found it.

Helga stamped her foot. "Have you nothing to say? When this is discovered, I will be forced to leave this place. My family will take the baby from me and leave it in the forest for the trolls."

Loftur put a hand around her waist and tugged her close. "Not to worry, my sweet. I'll make sure that never happens."

She looked up at him, cautious hope lighting her troubled face. "Do you mean it, Loftur? We will marry and raise this child?"

"Whatever you wish. We must talk about this more later. Come to my room after Compline and we will take joy of each other and our future."

Helga hugged Loftur tightly, burying her face against his robes. "I'm so happy," she said, her voice thick with tears.

He looked again up and down the corridor; still no one of importance was in sight. "Here, you must return to the kitchens to avoid suspicion until we settle our plans. I'll make you a shortcut." With a muttered incantation and a careful twisting of his fingers, he caused the stones and packed earth of the wall to become insubstantial and fade, creating a passageway from the corridor of the school to a pantry of the kitchens on the other side of a shared wall. "Now hurry along."

Helga pressed a kiss to his cheek and turned away, scurrying toward the kitchens. No sooner had she stepped into the passage Loftur had created than he reversed his spell. The stones and earth of the walls reappeared instantly. Solidly.

Satisfied, the young sorcerer dusted his hands and continued along the silent corridor to his Latin class.

A long time later, when the school was being demolished, a workman swung his hammer at the same wall between corridor and pantry. Stones and dirt fell away in a crumble of dust; when it cleared, the workman jumped back with a cry. For there, trapped in the tatters of the wall, was the rotted gray dress and skeleton of a woman, with the bones of a baby still visible in her belly.

CHAPTER

SEVEN

A few hours after leaving Grýla's cave, Magnús pulled the van into a grassy, flat area. He parked before a stone slab. Other buildings were visible at a distance, but his gift had led him to this spot.

The others looked skeptically at the slab, at the lack of any structure. Diwata consulted her phone again.

"Are you sure? Hólar University is supposed to be over there." She pointed at the cluster of buildings in the middle distance.

Magnús nodded, though he was not entirely sure himself. "I willed myself to the site in Hólar of the school that both Gottskálk and Galdra-Loftur attended. My gift tells me this is the place. Perhaps the current school was built on a different site?"

Ólafur scanned the stone slab and the otherwise empty field. A few young trees, grass, and the slab; Magnús had to admit to himself that this hardly looked like a school.

Diwata seemed unconvinced but pulled out the stone the witch Yrja had lent to her. "Okey doke, let's see if this will guide us to where we need to be."

"What are we looking for here?" Altair said.

"Good question," Magnús said. "We're following a hunch that there's a connection between this place and...whatever is going on with you. But we don't know exactly what we're after."

As the group climbed out of the vehicle, a chill breeze blew across the field, rippling the grass, stirring the leaves on the thin trees, before swirling around their heads and passing on.

Diwata shivered. "Ugh. Feel that? Something in that wind was unnatural."

Ólafur wandered closer to the copse of trees, apparently for a better look. He crouched and picked up an object from the grass: a mobile phone. "I'm guessing whoever left this was in a hurry to get away."

Altair joined him, took the phone, and examined it. "That's not a recent model I recognize. Still, you'd think whoever lost it would have come back to find their phone."

"If they were in a position to come back," Magnús said softly. "There's something dark here. Tread lightly."

He approached the slab, moving slowly and cautiously. Diwata muttered some words and gestured; the feeling of oppression eased slightly.

"A protection spell," she muttered. "Without doing a whole ritual thing, this is the best I can throw together on the move."

"It helps," Ólafur assured her, adding a small smile. Magnús exchanged a glance with Altair; the human's eyes were twinkling, and Magnús barely restrained a chuckle. He couldn't resist sending a mental jab at his cousin, though.

«Could you be any less subtle?»

Ólafur shot him an annoyed look but didn't respond.

Diwata held out Yrja's pendant at arm's length, and slowly rotated in place. "Something the Yule Cat thinks we need to see," she muttered, either to herself or to the wayfinder. "I can feel a small tug," she announced, taking a few small steps closer to the slab. Abruptly, her arm dropped toward the ground and she stumbled with a yelp. Ólafur rushed over to help her.

"What happened?" he asked.

"There was a strong pull on the stone," Diwata told him. "Straight downward."

Altair eyed the slab. "Could something be buried under the stone?"

"Possibly." Magnús crouched at the edge of the slab and carefully leaned down to touch the stone. Icy unease slid down his spine. "Something unpleasant is beneath, that's certain."

Diwata got out her galdrabók and sat cross-legged on the grass a short distance away from the slab. "Maybe I've got something useful in here," she muttered, beginning to thumb through pages. The others grouped themselves a few steps away, respectful of Diwata's possessiveness over her grimoire.

"Do you know any dvergur who might aid us?" Ólafur asked Magnús quietly.

"Dvergur?" Altair asked.

"You'd call them dwarves," Magnús explained. "Crafters and miners, mostly. They can find veins of ore, even move through solid rock. But no, Óli, I can't think of anyone who might come if we called. Perhaps if Bryndís asked, though..."

"Hey, that's a thought," Diwata said, apparently having heard them. "Dvergar magic. I think I remember..." She gingerly turned fragile-looking pages toward the back of the grimoire, then stopped and read one closely. She tapped the page with her fingertip. "Yes, this might help."

Diwata stood and brushed off the seat of her jeans. "Óli, would you get my bag from the back of the camper?" He hurried off toward the vehicle. Diwata muttered a few words as she looked at her book, perhaps practicing the difficult syllables of the dvergar tongue.

When Ólafur returned, she beamed a smile at him, then

dropped to her heels to rummage through the bag. She emerged with a small vial of what looked like reddish-colored sand. "The dvergar use this magic to find out if ground is solid or unstable. It helps if any area is volcanic and might have hidden weaknesses or fissures, or even lava." Carefully shielding herself from the slight wind, she unstoppered the vial and poured the contents into one palm. Ólafur held her grimoire for her as she reviewed the spell, then said the dwarvish words aloud. She spat onto the sand, then swept her hand out to cast it widely over the slab and surrounding area.

As the sand settled to the ground, it began to glow. Much of it was a dull red, but the sand covering a portion of the stone slab was bright blue. The area in blue was about three feet wide, forming a thick line that ran straight across the slab, at an angle to the stone itself.

"It's hollow under there," Diwata said, pointing to the blue. "And from the regular shape, it's got to have been made by hand. A tunnel or passageway, I'd guess."

"How do we get to it?" Altair asked. "Rent a jackhammer?"

Magnús shook his head. "Let me try something first." He called to mind the spell he'd created to help that hiker out of the troll pit. Was that just two days ago? Going down on his knees, he called on the light of Álfheimur. The glow began within his hands, bone-deep, and he heard Altair gasp. Picturing the runes in his head, he said the words in the tongue of the Álfar as the burn of his magic grew.

The stone under his hands shifted, then softened. It began to sag down into the earth below, revealing a tunnel beneath the slab covering. A stale smell of old air and dirt came out of the hole that formed. When Magnús released his spell, a portion of the slab had formed stairs down into the darkness.

"That was so cool," Altair said breathlessly. Magnús gave him a small smile, trying to look modest.

"Showoff," Ólafur muttered.

Altair came closer, crouching down to touch the reshaped stone. "So what did you do to it? I mean, it takes incredible amounts of heat to melt even quartz. Did you make the heat generate internal to the stone, or did it come from your hands?"

Magnús had to chuckle. "Honestly, I don't know how it works. It just...does."

Altair looked dissatisfied at the answer, but before he could press, Diwata joined them on her knees. She peered down into the revealed tunnel and shivered. "I really don't want to go in there."

"Agreed," Magnús said, "but I think that's exactly why we need to look. You can stay outside if you prefer."

"No way," Diwata said firmly. "It would be worse to wait out here, wondering if something has happened to you. If you're going in, so am I."

"I'm going, too," Altair said quickly. "But, uh...we'll be careful. Right?"

Magnús couldn't resist a quick squeeze of Altair's arm. "We'll take care of each other."

«Could *you* be any less subtle?»

Ólafur's return sarcasm was justified, Magnús decided, and let it go.

He pulled out one of his lightstones, whispering to spark its magic. Descending the stairs, he held the stone in his fingertips, angling its light. Diwata followed immediately behind him, then Altair, with Ólafur bringing up the rear.

The floor of the tunnel was packed earth. As they stepped into the corridor, Magnús laid a hand on the wall, made of pieces of stone fitted together neatly. "It's very cold to the touch, colder than just being underground would explain." The yellow glow of his stone revealed the corridor ended in just a few feet in one direction but continued into the darkness in the other.

Diwata grumbled, "Yrja's finder is pulling that way." She pointed to the blackness beyond the edge of Magnús's light.

Dagger in one hand, lightstone in the other, Magnús moved cautiously down the corridor. The cloying smell of dank earth continued, but at least it wasn't getting stronger. The walls of the corridor were mostly intact, though in a few places, stones had fallen to the dirt floor.

After about twenty yards, the corridor opened up into a small room, perhaps ten feet by fifteen. On one side of the room, rotted pieces of wood and some stones showed that a staircase had once led up. But the exit that way had collapsed or been covered over deliberately. There was no way up those stairs, and only the tunnel they had followed led back out. The room might have been used for storage, as stone ledges lined one wall. Otherwise, it was empty.

Diwata rotated in place slowly, arm outstretched, testing the guidance from Yrja's finder. "What we need," she muttered. "What the Yule Cat wants us to find."

The wayfinder twitched and pulled on its chain toward a section of stone wall to the right of the rotted staircase. Diwata followed the tugging to the wall, using her free hand to touch the stones. "I can feel colder air coming between these," she said.

Altair joined her, looking over the wall. "Some of these stones are fitted oddly. Almost like..." He ran his hand along the wall slowly, probing at the edges of some of them. "Ah!" he exclaimed, then worked his fingers in the gap between stones. He pulled, and a section of the wall shifted slightly.

"Careful!" Magnús hurried over, terrified Altair might accidentally bring down the stones on himself.

"Look here, it's made to come out." Altair showed Magnús some grooves that formed handholds and traced with his fingertips the perfectly straight lines that formed a rectangle about four feet by two feet. "There's something behind this. Maybe another corridor, or a room."

Diwata held up her pendant, then she nodded grimly. "That's the way Yrja's stone wants us to go."

Reluctantly, Magnús helped Altair to grip the section of wall and pull. The section slid toward them with the grinding sound of stone on stone, but it seemed surprisingly light for its bulk. When they lifted it out of the wall, they saw that stone pieces just a few inches thick were affixed to a wooden frame. Two people were enough to maneuver the hatch out and set it aside.

The four of them stood together, looking into the even darker opening they had revealed. An unpleasant smell of decay wafted toward them. Magnús's skin prickled; the warning of evil came on a breeze from that gloom.

"I think it's another tunnel, not a room," Altair said as he peered into the almost palpable darkness.

A chill numbed Magnús's fingers. "Thoughts?" he asked.

Altair chuckled nervously. "If there's something here, it'll be in a dark, hidden room."

Ólafur pulled out his dagger, similar to the one Magnús carried. "In," was all he said.

Magnús nodded and stepped through the opening in the wall. On the other side, a tunnel mostly formed of packed earth gave way in just a few feet to rough, natural stone walls.

"Whoever built this connected with some fissures or caves that already existed, I think," Altair said. "Look, you can tell from the angle the manmade corridor intersects the stone."

His voice trailed off as the group followed Magnús deeper. The light from his stone didn't seem to go very far at all. It was as if the blackness of the tunnel closed in around them.

A dry, earthy smell greeted their descent, along with a prevalent scent of decay. The tunnel sloped downward for a good thirty or forty feet but eventually opened to a larger cave with an earthen floor. The chill was even more pronounced below ground. To one side of the room, a wooden door had been set into the wall of the cave. On the other, an opening led still deeper into gloom.

Every instinct in Magnús pulsed there was danger here. He moved cautiously toward the door, put his hand to the wood, then snatched it away. "Frozen, like a block of ice."

A scrape sounded from the dark opening they had not explored. The group all whirled to face the area where the noise had come from.

Another scrape came, longer, like a foot dragging across dirt. Magnús repositioned himself between Altair and the darkness. He stretched out his hand, sending the yellow light as far forward as possible.

A third scrape, and then something glinted in the outer reach of the stone's glow.

"Give it back."

The words were low and menacing and came at them out of the opening in the cave wall. The voice was raspy and somehow slack. "Bring it back."

Another scrape, and the loose shape of a figure suggested itself against the black. Magnús thought he could see eyes staring at them. When he reached out mentally, though, he found absolutely nothing.

"Thieves. Always thieves." The voice sounded closer and angry. "So many came for it. But you! Somehow you took it."

With another dragging step, the figure moved far enough into the lightstone's glow that they could make out a man shape, wrapped in a long and tattered robe, head bare, eyes burning. It stretched a hand toward...

Toward Altair, of course. Magnús almost groaned.

"I haven't taken anything," Altair protested, stepping backwards, a slight tremble in his voice. "I've never been here before."

"Bring it back," the figure said, its voice increasing in intensity. "Bring. It. *Back*!" With each word, the volume grew and the shape expanded. The outstretched hand became a claw that reached for them.

Magnús slashed at the hand with his dagger, but it passed right through. Immediately a blast of wind hit them, so cold it made Magnús gasp, so strong it forced them back.

The lightstone fell from his hand and hit the cave floor, casting its glow up, illuminating the monstrous figure as it loomed over them. The hands reached again, and the group acted as one. They darted around the figure and toward where Magnús remembered the tunnel out to be.

The blackness had grown more absolute, though, and the chill was spreading, making his hands and face ache from the cold. He was completely blind, even though he should be able to see something from the fallen lightstone. They had been moving for longer than made sense, given the size of the cave. Hands held in front as he ran, he kept searching for the tunnel opening, but felt only cold, dark air.

Diwata stumbled and shouted, "We're trapped in its glamour, and its magic is more powerful than mine. I don't think I can get us out."

The shambling behind them grew close. A hoarse chuckle filled the air.

"Grimmi they name me, cruel shall I be, to the one who stole my book from me."

CHAPTER

EIGHT

Magnús pulled another stone out of his belt as they ran, trying to give them some light, but it didn't penetrate the oppressive gloom in which they found themselves.

"What *is* that monster?" Ólafur demanded.

"A draugur, I think. A ghost." Diwata sounded unnerved. "But really dangerous."

"Holy shit," Altair said. "Look."

Another shape had appeared ahead of them, a small cloud drifting in the air. It seemed to have its own internal, sickly glow. The suggestion of an arm, a hand, curving to beckon them, brought all four to a halt.

The ghost behind them laughed hollowly, the sound so close it might have its arms around them at any moment.

The smaller shape beckoned again, and with no other option, they ran toward it. A snarl came from behind them, then the scrape of dragging feet picked up speed to give chase. The wisp ahead glowed just brightly enough to show them the wooden door

49

Magnús had spotted when they first came into the cave. It passed right through the wood.

Magnús grabbed the handle, so cold it felt like his hand burned. With a prayer to the Allfather, he pulled hard and sighed gustily in relief when the door opened. They all pushed through into a smaller chamber. Magnús yanked the door shut behind them, then shook his hand to get some warmth back into it.

A crash rang through the air. The door shivered as if a mighty hand had banged against the wood with great strength. A second thump came, as loud as the first. Magnús held his breath, but the door withstood the blows.

He took a moment to look around, his lightstone revealing a room apparently formed from a cave about ten feet wide and deep. Instead of dirt, the floor had been covered in worked stones. Stone benches lined two walls. A smell in the air was less like the rot they had almost gotten used to, and more like...dried blood?

"The draugur was reaching for your bag," Ólafur said to Altair.

Altair shifted the ubiquitous satchel around, away from Ólafur's eyes. "What would a ghost want with notes on power plants?" he asked.

"I think we better take a look in there," Diwata said. "Maybe that crazy Yule Cat slipped something into it."

Magnús could see the struggle on Altair's face, but the young man said, "O-okay." He went to his knees and pulled the strap of the satchel over his head. He started to open it, but Diwata halted him.

"Let me," she said. "I've got some protective runes tattooed on, so it'll be safer."

Visibly forcing himself to relinquish the bag, Altair slid back a few feet on his knees. Diwata carefully opened the clasp and raised the top. She looked inside, and the others also leaned closer.

"What's this book?" she asked, lifting out a small volume. It was covered in a pink, floral fabric, and looked old and fragile.

Altair shivered. "That's my grandmother's diary. It's very precious," he said in an oddly toneless, flat voice. "I wonder how it got—"

The darkness seemed to swirl around Magnús for a moment, disorienting him. What were they doing again? He shook his head to clear it. Altair stood against a wall nearby, his satchel clasped closed and slung over his shoulder. Diwata and Ólafur were looking at each other, a slightly dazed expression on their faces.

Altair made a strangled noise like a scream choked back down before it could escape. Magnús whipped another stone from his pouch. Turning, he could see why Altair had reacted.

The figure that they'd followed through the door floated in the air before them. It was shaped like a human child, though no more than the size of a doll. What must have been its head was larger than the body. Its limbs were withered, and a few gray rags fluttered around the shape. The eyes were sunken and closed, though Magnús had no doubt it knew where they stood.

The group stood frozen in what Magnús now realized was a room with no other obvious exit than the door they'd come through. The door that kept them safe—for the moment—from a powerful ghost.

The floating child-shape hovered in the air, quite still for several long moments. Then it drifted toward the back of the chamber where a greenish glow from its body illuminated the rough stone cave wall.

Something glinted in the feeble light.

Diwata retrieved her finding stone and pointed it at the wall. "Tugging," she muttered and sucked in a nervous breath. She took a step closer to the wall and the child spirit. It didn't move, so she took another, leaning forward slightly to peer at the wall.

"It's a rune. I know this one, it means secret treasure."

The spirit drifted higher on the wall then, seemingly to give Diwata room. With a rattling inhalation, she reached a trembling hand to brush over the mark. "Yes. There's something here. Let me..."

She retrieved a dowel from her bag and scratched something against the wall. Then she muttered a short spell in what Magnús thought sounded like the dvergar tongue again. A piece of shale fell from the wall just where she had touched, crashing to the stone floor and making them all jump.

Magnús stepped forward, his lightstone illuminating the wall. Where the shale had been, an opening was revealed, perhaps a foot high. With another step, he shed yellow light into the opening.

Diwata, right by his side, gasped. The small space, perhaps two feet deep, contained a few items—a piece of black cloth, a small box, and a knife of some kind.

A high, creaky voice sounded in the still air of the chamber then.

> *"A present for my father*
> *to remind him of love's end*
> *From the son he never knew*
> *to repay him for love's end*
> *Triumph of the white student*
> *to reward him for love's end"*

Magnús and Diwata looked at each other, silently debating. Ólafur pointed up at the wisp of glowing light and said slowly, "I'm not sure, but...I think it wants us to take them."

"What have we got to lose?" Diwata muttered.

She thrust her hand into the opening and carefully took out the items. The dagger she passed to Magnús, handle first, then tried to examine the box and cloth in the weak light.

At that moment, another bang made them whirl. The child

spirit, whatever it was, drifted over their heads and toward the wooden door protecting them, for the moment, from the draugur.

"You've got to be kidding me," Altair muttered. "Does it want us to go back out there?"

The shade drifted lower and lingered a foot above the blade in Magnús's hand, hovered a moment, then floated up and right through the ceiling above them.

Magnús looked grimly at the others. "Did it just tell us we can use this dagger on the thing out there?"

"Not just a thing," Diwata said. "It called itself Grimmi. I think that's the ghost of Gottskálk, the priest who created the"— she stopped abruptly, looking at Altair—"the, uh, book of bad spells."

"The one Bryndís said another sorcerer tried to steal?" Altair asked. "Is that what the ghost was talking about when it said to 'bring it back'?"

"I don't know," Diwata said, "but the legend was that Galdra-Loftur called Gottskalk's spirit from Hel to force the dude to tell him what he had done with the spell book. Supposedly Galdra-Loftur failed to get what he wanted, but as I think about it, the story never said Gottskálk returned to Hel."

"What is the knife all about?" Ólafur asked.

Diwata examined the box and cloth she held. "There might be some clue here."

The box was a plain wooden one with a hinged lid and small gold clasp. The cloth was black, coarse in fabric, with a jagged edge as if it had been cut carelessly or in a hurry. Diwata opened the clasp of the box and raised its lid. A foul odor drifted out, making them all gag and cough.

Wiping her eyes dry after the fit had passed, Diwata extracted a folded piece of parchment; something else in the box was wrapped in a thick, white cloth. That was the source of the stench.

She squinted at the parchment, and Magnús brought his lightstone closer. With a nod from Diwata, he took the paper and unfolded it carefully. In the magical light, he translated the runic notations aloud. "Artifacts of the enemy of the Black School and its worshipful founder—the cloth of his imprisonment, the knife of his liberation, and a finger taken from his corpse."

"Eww," Altair said. "Is that what's in that wrapped bundle? The finger of some dead priest?"

"Not just a priest," Diwata said, her voice revealing excitement. "The enemy of the school. It has to be about Sæmundur. Remember? He was wearing a robe as he ran up the stairs, and he used an enchanted knife to slice off his shadow to trick Satan."

"The ghost kid did say something about a 'white student,'" Altair said.

"Ùtburður, I think," Diwata said. "The spirit of an abandoned or murdered child."

"Why would there be a word for that?" Altair moaned. "God, Iceland is weird. Are there that many abandoned or murdered children here?"

"It was a tough land," Magnús said. "And the human population was very poor. Illegitimate or unwanted children were sometimes left exposed in the wilderness by their mothers. The huldufólk took many in and raised them as servants before Queen Hildur put a stop to the practice. After that, we would try to take the abandoned ones to homes where we thought another human would give it shelter. But no doubt there were babies we didn't find alive in time."

"And if they died that way, some of them would come back as útburður," Diwata added. "But back to the point. If that is Sæmundur's dagger, and if it worked to defeat the Devil..."

"Then maybe it can defeat Grimey Gottskálk out there," Altair finished.

To Magnús, Ólafur said, "Is it just me or is it scary how quickly these humans seem to think alike?"

Diwata punched his arm. "Look, smartass. I'm short on tricks. If we're going to get out of here, I think that dagger is our best chance."

"Very well," Magnús said, drawing a deep breath. "Altair, stand back, please. Ólafur, if you'll open the door, I'll go through first and try to kill or at least distract the draugur. All three of you, run like mad to find the tunnel back the way we came."

Diwata stowed away the box again but hesitated with the ragged piece of black cloth. "Hold on. I've got a thought."

She folded the cloth like a bandana, then retrieved some items from her pouch. To Magnús, it looked like a stylus and a vial of ink. She opened the vial, dipped in the stylus, and sketched an elaborate rune on the cloth. After putting her materials away, she wrapped the cloth around her head, covering her eyes completely. She nodded sharply in satisfaction.

"Óli, you'll have to guide me through the door, I think," Diwata said, "but if I'm right, then follow me."

Magnús made sure Altair was safely back before he nodded to Ólafur to open the door. The ghost was several feet away, but it turned on them as soon as the door opened.

"Give it back!" it uttered hollowly. "Thief. I see you, I know you. Bring it back."

It moved toward them, but Magnús sprang forward to meet it. He was aware of Ólafur leading Diwata out of the small chamber, Altair right behind. Then Gottskálk reared before him, grown to monstrous size again.

"This way," he heard Diwata shout. "I can see through the spell hiding the tunnel opening. Follow me!"

The ragged hand of the ghost reached for Magnús, and he swiped fiercely at it with Sæmundur's dagger. A flash of silver fire illuminated the room as the blade cut through the outstretched hand and it fell to the floor as a shadow before dissolving into the dirt. A harsh, metallic smell filled the air.

Gottskálk shouted hoarsely and pulled back. Magnús pressed his attack, slashing viciously. The draugur retreated from Magnús's reach and intoned a spell. The earthen floor shook; Altair cried out as he stumbled, and Magnús felt the floor soften like quicksand beneath him. He leapt before it could go too soft, hurling himself at Gottskálk, knife hand raised.

As he came down on the dead bishop, he struck at its face. Silver flashed and left a deep wound. The odor of rotting garbage filled the air, making Magnús choke. The skin on either side of the wound caught fire, an argent burn that spread quickly to consume the ghost of Gottskálk the cruel.

Its furious scream sounded in Magnús's ears for long moments after the creature was gone.

He turned to see the tunnel opening was visible once more and that Altair and the others had made it out. He hurried after them, through the room with the destroyed staircase, down the stone corridor, back up the magicked stone steps, and to the camper van. Ólafur jumped into the passenger seat while Altair crowded with Diwata in the back; Magnús drove away at top speed. No one wanted to wait to find out if the ghost bishop was truly defeated or just regaining its strength.

"What did you do to guide us out of there?" Magnús heard Altair ask tightly. He glanced back; Altair was pale and trembling slightly, his jaw clenched. The terrors of the underground battle seemed to have hit him even harder than the others.

"Third Eye spell," Diwata said as if that explained everything. Her voice sounded excited. "I figured that Sæmundur's cloak might be a good medium for a rune to pierce illusions, and it was."

"What next?" Ólafur asked.

"We need to find a spot to regroup," Magnús said. "We aren't far from a cove I know."

"Drive fast, elf boy," Diwata said, sounding almost joyous.

"Between the cloth and that dagger, I think I've figured out how to free Altair!"

CHAPTER

NINE

Altair gnawed on his lower lip as Diwata opened her leather-bound grimoire and carefully laid it on a flat rock that jutted up at the edge of the black sand beach.

They'd chosen a location along a fjord—Magnús said it was called Skagafjörður—that was isolated and somewhat protected from the ever-present wind. The early evening air was fresh but chilly as the sun began its slide toward the horizon. A stiff breeze carried the briny scent of the sea to them. The shock of the evil ghost, the murdered child, the endless dark when they'd been trapped in the glamour...finally, his fears were easing in the fresh, clean air off the fjord.

"This is wild," Altair muttered, sketching a line in the black, wet sand with the toe of his shoe. "I've never seen a black beach before."

Magnús grunted and continued to place warding stones.

Ólafur called out from an area where tree limbs and other debris marked a tide line. "Altair, are you ready?"

He waved Altair closer to a ring of stones he'd assembled, about eight or nine feet in diameter. When Ólafur indicated he

59

should sit in the center of the ring, Altair grimaced. The wind, even partially blocked by a cliff, was still chilling. Not to mention that the black sand seemed slightly damp; his khaki-colored pants would look filthy when he stood up again. With a sigh, he sank onto his heels.

Diwata joined them in the stone ring, book tucked under one arm, the other stretched out as if testing the wind. She turned her body a few times and took a step to the right, then backward.

"There we go," she said. "Strong ley lines connect here."

She sat cross-legged, apparently unconcerned about the wet sand, and once again opened her grimoire. Folding his legs, Ólafur sank down elegantly next to Altair, leaving him between witch and elf. Magnús hovered at a slight distance, keeping watch on their camp while also shooting anxious looks Altair's way.

"What, uh, what are you going to do to me?" Altair asked.

Diwata was pulling items out of the bag at her waist; an opaque bottle, a piece of quartz, and a wooden dowel took their place next to the book. Reverently, she added Sæmundur's dagger to the assemblage, its carved black handle and silver blade seeming somehow more real than the items around it.

"A kind of magical brain surgery," Diwata said in a distracted tone, consulting her book and then shifting the position of the items. "Don't worry, we probably won't scramble any important thoughts."

This was delivered with a quick sideways smirk at Altair that made him tense.

"Dee, he's scared enough," Ólafur said. He patted Altair's hand. "Nothing so drastic, I promise. I'm going to look deep in your mind and try to find the source of this voice and sorcery that you and Magnús have experienced. Depending on what I find, Dee will use the Third Eye to locate exactly where the spell has been placed on you, then cut through it with Sæmundur's dagger."

"Will it hurt?"

Ólafur hesitated. "It shouldn't. But...we still don't know the exact nature of the sorcery. It may fight back."

Magnús abandoned his watch and stalked over. "This thing tried to kill me at least once. And it pushed me out of Altair's dream before."

"It did? Wait, you were in my dreams?" Altair was both alarmed at the threat and hurt at the idea. Magnús had spied on him asleep as well as reading his mind. Had he seen one of the dreams where Altair and Magnús...? The tips of his ears burned.

"I only touched the surface," Magnús said, crouching before Altair. "I didn't try to see your actual dream or interject myself. But this thing sensed me and pushed me away, hard."

And then Altair recalled waking from a dream, the echo of a shout in his ears, with the strange notion that Magnús had been there guarding him. From the first few moments together, Altair'd had a feeling Magnús would protect him. Was that only two days ago?

"Okay," Altair murmured, and Magnús looked relieved. "But Óli, if this sorcerer or whatever was able to force Magnús out of my head, why won't it do the same thing to you?"

"My special gift is with mind-speech. I'm more skillful than Magnús when it comes to these matters. I can project my thoughts farther and read human minds easily."

Altair bristled a bit. "Magnús *is* good at that. He reads me easily enough."

Ólafur gave him a small grin. "No insult intended. It's just a thing I can do naturally. Magnús has many skills I don't."

Somewhat mollified, Altair tried to compose himself. "I'm ready. What do you want me to do?"

"Altair has a good point, though," Magnús said. "This thing will probably fight back. Óli, are you sure you can keep Altair safe? We don't know enough."

"Well," Diwata said, "if you'd rather, we can do nothing and wait to see how it uses Altair to raise its armies before it kills him. That's a solid plan."

"Wh-what?" Altair asked, feeling a tremor begin in his hands.

"Honestly," Ólafur chided Diwata with a small shake of his head. A peaceful image of a meadow floated into Altair's mind and his trembling eased.

"It's just me helping so you don't react," Ólafur said. Then he looked at Magnús. "Cousin, trust me, I'll be very careful. If I don't think we can proceed safely, I'll stop. Dee is ready to counter any magical attack, and you're here to guard us as well."

"I want to do this," Altair said, looking up at Magnús. "I'm really creeped out at the idea somebody's been riding around in my head for who knows how long. But, uhhh...you'll be right here?"

Magnús looked deeply into his eyes. "The whole time. I promise."

Altair bit his lower lip and nodded quickly. Rolling his shoulders and shaking out his hands, he faced Diwata again. "I'm ready."

Diwata looked at her book once more, then wrapped the bandana made from Sæmundur's robe around her eyes. The effect was disconcerting—that pretty face with its eyes obscured behind a black band. Altair shuddered as she turned her head to face him. He felt sure she could somehow see him even through the blindfold.

"Yee-e-s," she said slowly, and the sound was somehow uncanny. "It's like with the draugur's illusion. I can see where the people who enchanted you hid the runes they branded on your skin."

"Brands?" Altair squeaked. "I've been branded? How would I not remember that?"

Shaking her head, Diwata then slowly rocked her body. With

the dowel in one hand and the quartz in the other, she struck the mineral three times, sharply, with the wood. Then she used the end of the dowel to scratch a pattern in the black sand, consulting her book frequently despite the blindfold. When she was satisfied, she set aside the dowel and quartz to pick up the bottle.

As soon as the stopper was out, Altair winced and wrinkled his nose. The smell coming from the bottle's contents was...awful.

"I know," Diwata said. "Some pretty gross stuff went into this. Shakespeare wasn't far off with his 'eye of newt' and 'tongue of dog' stuff."

"You didn't hurt a dog to make this, did you?" Altair protested. The idea of an animal suffering for him was repugnant.

Diwata held out a hand, palm up. "I solemnly swear no pet of any species was harmed in making this potion."

Magnús snorted skeptically from where he stood outside the circle, arms crossed. Altair heard the loophole as well, but he just huffed his acceptance. "Fine, go on."

Diwata tipped the bottle over the pattern she'd etched in the sand and let a thin stream of viscous, purple-brown liquid dribble over the lines. Instead of sinking into the sand, though, the substance glinted wetly in the trough of Diwata's rune. All the while, she muttered words that sounded vaguely Icelandic, but too softly for Altair to catch them. The rhythm of her speech seemed poetic.

When the pattern had been fully traced with the foul-smelling potion, she stoppered the bottle, set it beside her other tools, then stretched out her hands to Altair. He took them, surprised at how warm they seemed despite the breeze blowing up the beach.

She spoke again. "Nornir, your daughter seeks your blessing. Help me to see. Hermóður, son of Óðinn, god of messengers, help this man to speak his truth."

"Freyja, queen of cats, bright lady, bless our endeavor," Ólafur chimed in. "As magic was your greatest gift to the Æsir, bestow your gift on a child of Álfheimur who loves you."

Diwata took up her chant again. The pattern in the black sand glowed faintly with an indigo light that brightened steadily.

"Touch the liquid," Diwata instructed Altair. "Then dab it on each eyelid and on your throat."

Hesitantly, Altair leaned closer to the rune, nearly gagging at the smell. "Do I have to?" he asked pitifully.

"Yes," Diwata and Ólafur answered as one, then shared a small grin.

"You guys suck," Altair muttered, but he did as he was told. A glob of puce-colored goo, ice-cold to the touch, adhered to the forefinger he dipped into the pattern. He closed his eyes and dabbed once on each lid, then touched his throat.

"Now what—" he started to say, then threw back his head and screamed. His eyeballs were on fire, while a frozen hand clutched at his neck. Pain like he'd never felt roared through his body.

"Altair!"

He heard Magnús's shout, sensed Diwata shuffle back from his flailing arms and legs. He wanted to get to the water, to wash this awful pain away. He needed the water—

«Altair, let me in.»

Words rang in his head, and he dimly heard the fading echo of a bell, smelled ozone and seawater like an ocean breeze after a storm.

«Óli? Is that you?» Altair shivered and writhed in pain. «Help me, please. Get this shit off of me!»

Physical arms wrapped around him as well as the idea of mental ones as Ólafur held him tight. The pain was growing, his mind was in turmoil, ready to fly apart. He groaned again and felt fire rise up his gorge like bile, like acid.

«I can't take this. Please!» he begged.

«Got it!» Ólafur shouted in his mind. Aloud, the elf cried, "Diwata, now! Do you see it?"

"Whoever pulled this shit is a sick bastard," Diwata answered grimly. He felt her grip his shoulders. "Altair! Open your eyes. Look at me."

«Look at her,» Ólafur urged. «I'm keeping you from the worst of the pain»—*What?*—«but it's strong magic. Yours is stronger. Let Diwata help your magic.»

Tears streaming down his cheeks, Altair forced his eyes open. His throat was raw. Could it be bleeding inside? He'd never known such agony existed. His arms felt like they were breaking. And his feet? What was wrong with his feet?

Diwata leaned over him, Sæmundur's dagger in one hand. She gripped it so the blade pointed down. Silver danced along its length, or was that his tears? Words fell from her lips and Altair could almost see them, dripping blue fire. Over her shoulder, Magnús was clutching his hair, looking wild and desperate.

The pain *cracked*. That was the only word for it. Something inside him reached through the wall of agony, trying to get free. It pulled toward Diwata, toward the words she was chanting. Ólafur had picked up her spell and repeated the words directly into Altair's mind. The pain shivered and spasmed, trying to hold itself together.

A cage! Altair saw it suddenly as an image in his mind. The pain was a cage of black iron, tight around his throat, piercing his eyes. The black iron was his body, but it burned. Diwata came at him with the dagger, barely touching its point to the hollow of his throat, where the lock to the cage branded his skin. Light blazed from the point, heating the iron of the lock to a red-orange glow that continued to climb toward white-hot pain.

He couldn't take this. It had to end.

He screamed, and whatever it was he screamed was the same

thing Diwata was chanting, the same thing Ólafur was saying to his soul.

"I hope this hurts, you bitch," Diwata said. Altair flinched from her words, but she shook her head. "Not you. The witch on the other end of this spell. They built a cage with shame and fear. Even being this close to it makes me feel terrible. Oh, Altair, what you've had to—Wait, I can feel the flaw, the place to slice. There!"

She pressed again with the dagger, this time nicking his skin, but it didn't matter because he heard a scream of pain and fury in his mind, a scream that sounded familiar somehow. *Willa?* And then the dagger blazed so brightly it melted into the lock to his cage until it shattered.

He was free! Free! Oh god, the pain was gone and he was free!

His eyes—the burning had stopped. His throat was soothed. He threw back his head to cry in relief and what came out was...

Was...

The cry of a bird! He opened his eyes, and he was hundreds of feet above the black sand beach. So sharply he might have been standing next to them, he could see Ólafur's stunned expression, Diwata's glee and amazement.

And next to them was Magnús, arms spread wide, joy on his face. Altair wheeled and turned, his wings effortlessly catching the strong sea breeze.

His wings? Craning his neck left and right, wings of brown and gold feathers stretched to either side, adjusting minutely to the currents as he banked and flew. He shouted in astonishment and heard his shrill cry echo over the waves. Feet tucked into his body, Altair soared even higher.

This was glorious! He might be a mile above the fjord. The pain was nothing but a memory now. He had never felt more himself in his entire life. The coastline stretched away, his sharp eyes noting every lap of an icy wave on the black shore, the way shadows stretched behind jutting rocks as they ran from the setting sun. Fish in the fjord below, even a smaller bird. These were his rightful prey, because he was... He was...

What am I? He faltered in flight, his body plummeting for a moment until instinct took over again and he fell into a controlled dive.

«Altair!» The voice was in his head, and he knew it for Ólafur, reaching out. «You are a skin changer. A golden falcon!»

A falcon?

«YES,» he thought fiercely. «I am the Falcon!»

He thought it at Ólafur. At Magnús whom he loved, at the witch Diwata, whose mind could not hear but whose heart bled happiness for him. She wiped tears from her face as he wheeled in the setting sun and again screamed his joy to the winds.

«*—Heir of Veðurfölnir—*»

The warmest voice Altair had ever heard suddenly sounded in his head. More loving even than his own mother's voice had been.

«*—At long last, come to me, son of my loyal Fálki. Come north to learn who you are.—*»

CHAPTER

TEN

INTERLUDE

"Then said Gangleri: What other remarkable things are there to be said about the ash? Hár answered: Much is to be said about it. On one of the boughs of the ash sits an eagle, who knows many things. Between his eyes sits a falcon that is called Veðurfölnir. A squirrel, by name Ratatoskur, springs up and down the tree, and carries words of envy between the eagle and Níðhöggur."

— *FROM* THE PROSE EDDA: Norse Mythology by Snorri Sturluson

ELEVEN

Magnús watched in awe as the falcon that had been Altair flew and wheeled, dove down and soared up again through the crisp air. The sun sat low on the horizon, casting a golden glow over the beach and the fjord. The light made the falcon stand out in sharp relief against the sky, as if it were more real than anything else Magnús could see.

In solitary times, he had sat on the sides of cliffs, just watching the birds of Iceland fly to the hunt and return to their nests. Never had one so clearly flown for joy.

The streak of brown and gold threw itself at the sea, then spread its wings again to skim above the waves. Its shrill cry resonated in Magnús's soul. The breeze curled his hair around his face; he brushed it aside impatiently, eyes burning as he watched the falcon conquer the evening sky.

Seeing Altair in pain had been awful. Excruciating. Diwata had kept Magnús from interfering with a fierce glare he could feel through her blindfold. Ólafur had held Altair, trying to keep him still as his feet beat against the sand and he moaned in pain.

"Diwata, now! Do you see it?" Ólafur shouted.

"Whoever pulled this shit is a sick bastard," Diwata answered grimly. She leaned forward to grasp the pain-ridden human by his shoulders. "Altair! Open your eyes. Look at me."

Then Magnús saw it, too. A cage made of shadows contained Altair's body. It grew thickest in the area of Altair's throat, coalescing into a swirl of black lines at the hollow. Through the mass, he could somehow still see a sigil glowing in lines of red on the skin of Altair's throat.

The brand that trapped him.

Diwata placed one palm over the symbol, pointed the blade, and shouted some words over and over. Ólafur's teeth were bared in a grimace as he struggled to hold Altair. Something swelled inside Altair's body; Magnús could feel it pulse outward, but he couldn't see anything.

One more time, Diwata shouted her words, pressing Sæmundur's dagger to Altair's throat. The black cage exploded silently; she and Ólafur flew backwards and away from Altair as if tossed by a hurricane.

Altair threw back his head and screamed, but the scream was the cry of a bird. In a span of seconds, his arms became wings, his feet talons. And then an enormous gold and brown falcon, its wingspan easily twenty feet, shot into the sky. The shreds of Altair's clothing lay forgotten in the sand, inside the stone circle.

Now Magnús couldn't look away. "Gods of Earth and Air," he breathed. "He's glorious."

Ólafur and Diwata limped closer to Magnús. Ólafur said, "I've never felt anything like it. The war in his mind, from that thing branded on his skin and what was inside him...I don't know how he survived that."

Magnús turned furious eyes upon his cousin. "If it was that bad, why didn't you stop it? You promised he'd come to no harm."

"Shut it, elf," Diwata barked at him. "You weren't in there. The pain was vital to it all. Altair couldn't stop, any more than a woman in contractions could keep her baby inside. Altair suffered, but he had to move through it to be free."

"Your chant," Ólafur said to her. "I've heard that used when one of my horses is throwing a foal. It's a charm for an easy birth."

Diwata shrugged. "It was the only thing I could think of."

"Well, it worked," Ólafur told her warmly.

Magnús rolled his eyes and looked up again to find Altair in flight. For an alarming moment, he couldn't spy the mighty bird. Instinctively, he reached out with his mind as he would to one of the huldufólk. «Altair? Where are you?»

«I'm coming.»

The answer was sharp and clear. It didn't carry the mental signatures of one of Magnús's own kind, but the voice was piercing. Strong. Even not having heard it before, Magnús would know its owner anywhere.

Out of the setting sun, a winged shape dove toward them. For a panicked moment, Magnús thought the falcon had lost control and would crash to the beach. But its wings twisted to cut the air, its talons extended, and it was Altair who stood on the black sand, panting.

A very naked Altair.

Diwata snorted but kindly turned her back. Ólafur grinned. "I'll get you something from my pack," he said.

Seemingly unaware of his nudity, Altair looked up at Magnús, his golden eyes gleaming, as if lit from within.

"Who or what is Veðurfölnir?" he demanded.

"Uh, what?" Magnús asked stupidly. He was distracted by the miracle that stood before him, a skin-changing human. A human who had healed from the mystic brand that had been burning on his skin, because his throat was now smooth and unmarked. As was his chest, where the final scars from the ghoul cat's death throes had vanished.

"Veðurfölnir," Altair repeated. "It called me the 'heir of Veðurfölnir.'"

"What did?" Ólafur asked as he rejoined them, a shirt and pair of pants in his hands. Altair didn't even seem to realize he was naked, but he took the clothes and pulled them on, eyes never leaving Magnús's face.

"There was a voice when I was flying up there. Not the bad one. This one loves me. It said I'm the heir of Veðurfölnir, it called my father its 'loyal Fálki,' and said I have to go north to learn who I am."

"That word. Veðurfölnir. It...sounds familiar," Magnús said. He helped Altair settle the shirt on his shoulders. "Ólafur—"

"I know." His cousin snorted. He already had a smartphone in his hands and was typing. A few seconds later, his jaw dropped. When he looked up, his face was full of wonder.

Silently, he held out his phone so everyone could see the image of an old engraving. An enormous, stylized ash tree spread to the sky and sunk roots deep into the earth. A snake coiled among the roots, a squirrel ran up the trunk, and atop its lofty crown, an eagle spread its wings.

And above the eagle, eye to eye with its wings spread, was a falcon.

Magnús read the accompanying text aloud. "The falcon Veðurfölnir serves the great Eagle, bringing it news." Awestruck, he looked down at Altair. "I know of only one Eagle in our legends. It is Gammur, the Landvættur who guards the north of Iceland."

Altair blinked, twice. "Wait, I'm supposed to be, what, some kind of servant to a magic eagle?"

Ólafur sucked in a breath, sharply. "Please, don't be so callous, Altair. Gammur is one of our most revered figures. It is one of the Four, you see? The Four who have protected Iceland from time immemorial. Before the Norsemen arrived, before the huldufólk walked these lands, there were the Landvættir."

Altair blushed. "I'm sorry, Óli. I don't mean to be rude. But, what the hell? I mean, servant to a kind of god? *Me*?"

"You," Magnús said, conviction growing. "I knew you were something more than human. All the signs were there, the way you could hear our mind-speech, the way you could see my magic. The sorcery around you—I think its purpose was to keep your true nature hidden, from yourself and from the world. It's why the prophecy named you, and why you are tied to the very fate of—"

"Magnús! No, you'll trigger an attack!" Ólafur cried.

"I don't think so," Diwata said, her shrewd gaze on Altair. "Look. He isn't seizing or even reacting. It was the struggle between his own magic and the sorcery done to him that made him convulse and nearly die before. When he broke free of the spell, the magic inside him won."

Altair looked around at the three people watching him carefully. "Prophecy? Seizing? *Die*? I mean...what the actual fuck?"

Carefully, Magnús explained. He spoke hesitantly at first, watching for some sign of the convulsions that had wracked the young human before. But it seemed Diwata's assessment was correct. Altair, though alarmed and perhaps in shock, seemed not to react otherwise.

"I'm sorry we had to lie to you," Magnús concluded. "We came as close to the truth as we could, without bringing on another seizure."

Altair looked a bit faint. "I think I need to sit down."

Magnús helped him to lower onto the black sand, then folded his long legs to sit next to Altair. "Do you have any questions?"

Altair barked out a pained laugh. "Do I have *questions*? Oh boy, do I." He put a hand to his forehead. "I'm dreaming this, right? I didn't have a life-threatening seizure I don't remember.

I'm not a figure in a prophecy of doom and gloom. I'm not the long-lost servant of a god. And *I didn't turn into a fucking falcon and fly!*"

"He's taking it well," Diwata observed dryly.

Magnús shushed her and took Altair's hands. "You flew. You spread wings and you took to the sky like you belong there. That's the single most important thing to focus on."

Altair contemplated their joined hands. In a weak voice, he asked, "Do you really think this can all be true?"

"I do. You are special, Altair Fálkason."

Altair stiffened. "The voice—Gammur?—it called my father Fálki loyal. How could that be? My father abandoned us when I was little. What kind of loyalty is that?"

"I don't know," Magnús said honestly. "There's only one way to find out. We must go north and seek the Eagle."

"New moon is tomorrow," Diwata murmured. "We're running out of time to figure this shit out."

"Maybe you should open the Hidden Ways?" Ólafur suggested.

"I don't know enough about where to take us, though," Magnús said. "And I'm not sure the humans could survive in there long enough to search."

Ólafur crouched and put a hand on Altair's knee. "The voice you heard. It called you. Can you feel the direction of the summons?"

"I...I don't know."

Rising to his feet, Altair dusted the black sand off his trousers. He turned in place a few times, squinting out over the waves, then back along the beach. "There's something... I can almost hear it call..."

"Close your eyes," Magnús suggested. "Don't try to force a connection, just let yourself be still. That's right. Breathe softly. Listen to the wind."

They watched Altair turn his face this way and that, slowly. The setting sun gilded his body, lit his reddish hair, then flashed in his golden eyes as he opened them wide.

"That way!" Altair's hand shot up to point, roughly northwest of where they stood. "It's there."

"Good job," Ólafur praised, and Altair flushed.

"Guess we're driving more," Diwata sighed. "I want shotgun this time."

They had just begun to load themselves back into the car when Magnús paused. Light flickered at the edge of his vision.

"Wait a minute," he said, holding up a hand. "There's something..."

His vision blurred, then words formed before his eyes. Golden letters, as if written on the wind.

"Karl is writing to me," he muttered, recognizing the letters were scrawled on the mirror he'd enchanted. The letters were out of focus, fuzzy... Perhaps his friend was too far away for the spell to reach him?

Without knowing why he did it, Magnús reached out for Altair's hand. As soon as their fingers intertwined, energy pulsed between them and the golden letters jumped into sharp relief. They spelled a single word.

HELP

CHAPTER

TWELVE

When they clasped hands, cold fire ran down Altair's arm and, from his fingers, spilled into Magnús. He had no idea what it meant, though he felt Magnús stiffen in alarm.

"Karl is in trouble," Magnús said. "I need to get to him."

"Karl! Where is he?" Diwata demanded.

"He's within range of the message spell," Magnús said, craning his neck around. "But he could be in any direction."

"Can you ask Karl for more information?" Altair asked, unsure of what was going on but sure of Magnús's frantic response.

"I never figured out how to send a message back to the mirror." Magnús sounded frustrated, but the words made no sense to Altair. "I should have taken the time. Dammit."

Diwata peered thoughtfully at Altair in a way that made him nervous. "Messenger," she muttered. "Or more, who knows? But messages.... Yes, that fits. Worth a try, anyway."

"What is?" Altair asked.

"Óðinn uses his ravens to gather information. Huginn and

Muninn, Thought and Memory. The Allfather sends them out to observe and to report to him on all the sordid details of life in Miðgarður. Got it, bird boy?"

"Um, maybe."

"It wouldn't be very useful to know what just two birds saw, though, no matter how far they flew. Some legends have it that Huginn and Muninn gather their intel from the other birds they encounter and then summarize for Óðinn at the end of the day."

Despite his own shock and Magnús's agitation, Altair had to smile. "So they composed a listicle for him? Like, the top ten shenanigans of the day? Ow!"

Diwata had punched his arm. "Don't be salty. But...yeah, probably something like that. Your Falcon exists to do the same thing for Gammur. You're a messenger god. Or demigod."

"I'm a what now?"

"Keep up. You're apparently the messenger charged with gathering information and bringing it to Gammur, just like Huginn and Muninn. So I'm thinking, like them, you probably talk to birds and get all the juicy gossip so you can fly off and share it with Gammur. Shit, you probably can command birds to help you."

Altair's heart thudded painfully, and a wave of dizziness made him sway. Diwata peered at him intently. "You all right, bird boy? All of a sudden you don't look so hot."

"Altair?" Magnús tightened their mingled fingers. "What's wrong?"

"The birds..." Altair said, hating the way his voice quivered. "When we were at the university. Those seagulls died for us because I called them."

"I think...the birds were probably just trying to help us."

Altair nodded, not trusting himself to speak.

"It fits," Diwata said. "The birds know you and want to help you, even when you didn't know what you are."

"Awesome, I'm a bird god. Now what?"

"Now, dummy, you ask them to help find Karl."

Ólafur moved up to stand behind Diwata. "Of course. It makes sense now."

"What does?" Magnús asked.

"The way Altair has picked up Icelandic. Haven't you noticed that we've been speaking it more and more, yet Altair has been able to track it, even speak it."

"Have I? I didn't realize."

"Nor did I," said Magnús. "I suppose we switch languages so frequently that I hadn't paid enough attention. Let me try something." He stepped back from Altair but held on to his hand. "Can you understand this? 'Heiði hana hétu, hvars til húsa kom, völu velspá, vitti hon ganda.'"

"Very funny," Ólafur snarled.

Altair squeezed his eyes closed, replaying the words in his head. "Heithi they named her who sought their home, the wide seeing witch, uh, smart in magic?"

"'Magic-wise' is the usual translation," Diwata said. "You're right, Óli. I hadn't noticed either. It's brilliant, isn't it?"

This to Altair, who was feeling more unsettled than excited. "I...suppose?"

"So?" Diwata gestured vaguely at a flock of birds passing overhead.

"Talk to them?" Altair answered skeptically. "About what?"

"The weather." Diwata threw up her hands. "Gah! What is it with men? Ask the birds if they've seen Karl!"

Sighing, Altair looked up and into Magnús's eyes. "This is crazy," he muttered, "but no crazier than me thinking I can fly."

"You did fly," Magnús said resolutely. "You are a skin changer who turned into a falcon. As for the rest, I don't know. But see it through my eyes, Altair. See your wings."

The tickle by Altair's left ear was more pronounced than it had been the first day he met Magnús, but again, he smelled ancient snow, heard the creak of glacial ice. Magnús's blue eyes grew even larger, until Altair felt as if he were slipping into a still pond of cool water...

And gasped as he saw *himself*. Saw himself writhing in pain—*am I really that skinny?*—saw the moment arms became wings and a motherfucking *falcon* flew up into the sky from where he had thrashed on the sand just moments earlier.

«It's all true,» Magnús said in his head. «I don't know what it means to be the heir of Veðurfölnir, but we will find out together. I promise. But right now, please help to find my friend.»

Altair inhaled deeply and nodded. None of this was what he'd signed up for, when he accepted the grant. But he couldn't escape the reality, either. He was traveling with two elves and a witch, he could grow wings and fly, and Magnús wanted his aid. Karl was obviously important to him.

How important? an unworthy part of his brain asked, but he shunted it aside. Magnús needed his help.

And wasn't that a kick in the head, after how many times Magnús had already been there to help Altair?

"I'm ready," he said to Magnús. "Show me again. I only saw Karl the once, and I think I need to be exact."

An image filled his head, of the stocky man with russet red hair and a thick beard of a slightly darker red. Karl looked more rugged than handsome to Altair, more solid than gym muscled, and, in Magnús's memory, tended to chew on his lower lip.

"Got it," Altair mumbled and looked around the sky above his head. Dropping Magnús's hand, he took a few steps to a level space that was clear of rocks and slowly rotated himself as he watched the skies.

Soon a pair of common eiders on their way to hunt—*and how did I know that?*—were winging overhead. Words rose from Altair's belly, making his heart thump loudly as they climbed to his throat. Then he opened his mouth to let out the words.

Immediately the ducks banked and flew around him in circles, crying out their gladness and welcome. It wasn't language that he heard so much as sensations. The joy of wind rustling their neatly arranged feathers, the glint of sunlight on water, the bond between the pair that identified them to one another in a hundred tiny ways.

He sensed himself through their eyes as an ancient and beloved power, too long missing from their migration paths. They were eager to honor him, eager to be of service. Altair felt himself blush at their excitement.

Responding in the same way they communed with Altair, he described Karl and asked the eiders for news. They hadn't seen such a human, but they would spread the word among raven and wren, arctic tern and black-backed gull, and all the other kinds of birds, and bring back news.

Altair smiled as the eiders quacked happily and flew off. He noticed the other three watching him. Diwata looked amused, Ólafur thoughtful, and Magnús proud enough to burst.

"Um, they say they'll ask around and get back to us," Altair said.

"Well done," Magnús said. He stepped closer and threw an arm around Altair's shoulder. "You are a wonder."

Altair felt chills run up his back and down his arms from the contact. *Don't be stupid, he's just being friendly.* But he couldn't help leaning into the tall elf, breathing in his scent of birch and fresh ice. It would kill him to leave Magnús, when it was time to return to Boston.

Magnús stiffened next to him and dropped his arm. "You're going back?" His voice sounded rough and shocked.

"Well, I have to... Hey! You said you wouldn't read my mind anymore without permission." Altair stamped his foot. "Dammit, Magnús."

Ólafur hurried over. "It wasn't his fault, Altair. You're broadcasting your thoughts right now. You have to get a handle on this or every álfar in a dozen miles will hear."

"Even I got some of that," Diwata threw in. "You're sending out signals like a satellite radio station."

"Uh, what?" Altair asked, feeling stupid. He looked at Magnús to apologize.

"No need, little bird," Magnús said before Altair could speak. "This is something álfar children learn to control at an early age."

Ólafur grinned wickedly. "Some learn later than others. Isn't that right, Cousin?"

Now Magnús was the one to redden. "You promised never to bring that up again."

Diwata had finished gathering her spell ingredients and sauntered over. "Oh, this I've got to hear."

"Óli—" Magnús said in a warning tone, but it was too late.

"Magnús has always been fascinated by you humans," Ólafur said. "Even when he was a tyke of thirty or forty, he would wander away from the town to look at how you lived, what you ate, what you read." His sly grin spread. "And what you did in bed."

"Oh no," Altair gasped. Magnús hid his face in his hands.

"Oh yes," Ólafur continued gleefully. "A fisherman and the son of one of the merchants, wasn't it, Cousin? Magnús was curious when he spotted them slipping away from a gathering and followed them to a secluded glen. Invisibly, he crept closer as they embraced. The little fiend watched them clutch fiercely and fumble to move aside their clothing. So intent was Magnús to learn what the men were up to that he didn't remember his training. And so we were all treated to a front row lesson in human sexuality until Lady Bryndís got his attention."

Diwata was purple with laughter. Altair couldn't help grinning. "That must have been so embarrassing," he murmured.

"You can't imagine," Magnús said with a sigh. "Óli's brother Vörður even composed a verse about it. Which Óli will *not* be repeating"—he shot his cousin a fierce glare—"unless he wants me to tell you about that one trollwife who liked to bathe in a rock pool...?"

"Truce!" Ólafur said, holding up his palms as he laughed.

Altair flicked another glance at Magnús. It would be as awkward as anything Magnús had broadcast if Altair had one of those dreams about the elf... Hurriedly, he tried to picture a white piece of paper to stop that train of thought.

"So, uh, how do I learn to control this?" Altair asked.

Ólafur cocked his head. "Actually, whatever you just did was exactly the right idea. Your thoughts blanked out before they got to what you dream about."

Altair squeaked in alarm, then flushed at the horrible sound that had just come out of him. "I didn't dream anything. Never. I mean, of course I do, sometimes, but I haven't had... I mean, there's just—"

"Relax," Diwata said as she coaxed Altair to sit on a nearby rock. She had pulled some more of her baked goods from a sack in the van and passed them around. "Anyone with eyes can see you're into Magnús. He's a silver edged fox, of course you're attracted to him."

"He isn't that good looking," Ólafur muttered as he came to crouch next to Altair. "You'll find this easy, I suspect. You seem to be a natural. All you have to do is practice picturing yourself in a completely white room, with no doors or windows. No space for any stray thought to creep out into the world. It's tricky to maintain at first, but pretty soon it will become automatic and you won't have to think about it consciously."

Altair listened as Ólafur gave him Telepathy 101. He was aware all the time, though, of Magnús watching the sky anxiously. Ólafur had just begun to explain about the sigils that let them send their thoughts farther when Magnús yelled.

"The ducks are returning," he said, pointing, but Altair realized he didn't even have to look. His awareness of the eider pair, accompanied by a wild swan, was like a wisp of song heard on the breeze. He rose and turned toward the approaching birds.

The eiders wheeled overhead, but the swan alit on the rock Altair had been using. It fanned its white wings to steady itself, uncomfortable on a hard surface and longing for its pond. It had no wish to appear untidy and graceless before the Honored Emissary. The swan trumpeted its discomfort.

Altair hurried closer to the unhappy bird. "Thank you for coming, beautiful one. Our need is great, and you grace us with your presence."

"What's that sound coming out of Altair?" he heard Diwata murmur.

Ólafur said softly, "It's almost the same as the swan's call. I can tell there's intent to Altair's cry, but I don't know what he might be saying."

Magnús shushed them both. Altair was grateful because he could hear the swan's message more clearly without distractions. The bird told him as much as it knew, then crouched to leap into the welcoming air—*light chill, over the water, the air rises...there!*— and flapped its wide wings to catch the wind.

Altair raised a hand in farewell, calling out his thanks to swan and eider as they winged away.

"Did they tell you anything?" Magnús asked, his voice tight with worry.

"The swan saw Karl. Well, it *thinks* he was the man we want. Humans kind of look alike to—"

"Where is Karl? Is he in danger?"

"Trolls have him, somewhere that way," Altair said, pointing north. "I think that's what the swan saw—three of them, big things, foul air around them, won't stay still long enough to build a nest even though they have crags that would be perfect."

"Troll," Ólafur confirmed.

"Where?" Magnús asked, rage tinging his voice. His face transformed into something fierce and determined, and Altair suddenly pitied the trolls—or anyone—that Magnús turned his rage upon.

"I'm having trouble figuring it out in human terms. There are rocks piled beside a fjord that look like pipe organs. Then farther north, there's a double fjord between us and the trolls. Karl was pushed into a cave in some hills close to an orange and red and...and *wrong* building." Altair flushed. "I'm not sure I got that part right. The birds can see colors I don't have a word for, but they don't like this structure."

Magnús and Ólafur looked at each other and shared a firm nod. "The old lighthouse on Tröllaskagi," Magnús said. "I don't know about the bodies of water between us, but the tip of the peninsula is about forty miles northeast of us."

Ólafur pulled out his phone and called up an aerial view in a mapping app. He pinched and expanded the image, then nodded. "Yes, it fits. I see the Staðarbjörg basalt columns, then there are two fjords close together on the way to the point of land where the lighthouse sits."

"Fine," Magnús said, his jaw set. "You both take Altair to find the Eagle, and I'll go free Karl."

"That's foolish," Ólafur said. "You can't possibly handle three trolls alone."

"And you don't have to," Altair protested. "We should stay together, tackle this as a group."

"It's my fault Karl is in this situation. If I hadn't set aside the investigation into the trolls, I'd be there now."

"You stopped looking for the trolls because the Nornir and Bryndís told you to," Diwata said. "Karl is my friend, too, but I know he's smart and he's well trained. He's in trouble for sure, but he went into this with eyes open. So now we'll go help him."

"It's too dangerous—" Magnús started to say, but Altair cut him off.

"*All* of this is dangerous. You just said there's a prophecy I'm going to die if you aren't there. So, we stay together. Period."

Altair couldn't believe the words coming out, but he knew he was right. Magnús opened and closed his mouth, eyebrows drawn together, as he seemed to be working on a new objection.

"Okay, we have a direction," Diwata said firmly, as if the matter were decided. She stared hard at Magnús, who looked troubled but swallowed any further arguments. With a sharp nod, she folded her arms. "Good. Now we need a plan. I have trouble believing that trolls would randomly claim a site called Tröllaskagi. And tomorrow morning there's a new moon rising. I think this is a trap."

CHAPTER

THIRTEEN

Not long after midnight, Magnús surveyed the rocky seacoast through night vision binoculars that had been a gift from Karl. Wind whipped his hair, and he pulled it together into a loose knot. Even with his race's natural resistance to temperature extremes, the air was cold and damp.

He hoped Altair was warm enough.

The landscape was dark even to his keen eyes, though the binoculars helped. But the moon was new, which sent alarm bells through his being.

This was the beginning of the prophesied day.

The lighthouse stood on the edge of a cliff just as he recalled, its bright coloration somewhat visible even in the pitch-black night. The waves of the Iceland Sea crashed against rocks, sending up spray he could feel at this distance. At his back, some of the tallest mountains in Iceland stood sentinel.

Relatively few tourists left the Ring Road to visit the Tröllaskagi Peninsula. As a result, no cars were parked near the lighthouse this night. One blessing at least: they wouldn't have to worry about innocent people getting hurt.

Magnús wished he knew how Karl had come to be captured, and whether more of the missing hikers were in the troll den. Diwata was likely right that this was some kind of trap, and they had debated how to proceed during the drive north. Ólafur had wanted him to open the Hidden Ways to get inside, which was possible in theory but would leave Magnús useless if they were overwhelmed. Altair had suggested waiting for the day, but then they would never be able to draw the trolls out of their caves. Fighting inside was a guarantee for disaster. Finally, they decided their best option was to attack at night, to lure the trolls into the open, and confuse them.

Diwata scratched runes on pieces of driftwood, consulting her grimoire by the light of a small, battery powered lantern as she worked. She muttered, "May no outside sources interfere with my blessings. May nothing penetrate my wall of protection..."

Altair scanned the horizon, looking for night-flying seabirds who might be able to give them more information. Ólafur had become invisible and moved forward, keeping his connection with Magnús's mind open. His cousin was approaching an opening in one of the hills that Altair said matched what the swan had shown him. As far as they knew, that was the way into the troll den. The bird had told of three trolls, but they had no way of knowing what else might be lurking within the caves.

Magnús stowed his binoculars and got to his feet, ready for his part. The plan was to lure out the trolls, giving Ólafur a chance to slip inside. He would use Diwata's wayfinding stone to locate and, hopefully, free Karl. Magnús's pouch was full of as many enchanted stones as it could carry, and Sæmundur's dagger hung ready from his belt. Diwata would support Magnús with her spells.

Altair was under strict instructions to hang back, since his safety was paramount to the fate of Iceland. But if he could persuade any birds to help, he would do so.

"Hold on," Diwata whispered, standing from her work. She approached Magnús and gestured for him to hold out his hands. With a stylus she had blackened in a small fire, she sketched some runes on the back of each hand, muttering an invocation to Freyr as she did so. When the runes were done, she leaned in closely.

"That's the best I can do in this darkness," she whispered. "For luck in battle and for speed. I made a protection amulet for Óli before we left Hamarinn, but I don't have the materials or time to make one for you. May Freyr guide you to victory, Magnús Bryndísarson."

"Thank you, Diwata Pétursdóttir," Magnús said formally. "Your gifts are great."

"Well, don't make it sound like this is goodbye, elf boy," she said, then elbowed him in the side. "You'll be fine."

"Magnús," Altair whispered, joining them. His anguished voice made Magnús want to pull him close.

Instead, Magnús replied gently, "You heard our witch. Remember, she's a seer."

"I want to do more to help." Altair scanned the horizon again. "I can't find any birds. I don't know if they all nest at night or what. Are you sure I shouldn't turn into a falcon again and come with you?"

"Absolutely not," Magnús said. "At best, any birds would provide a distraction. They couldn't harm a troll. And you're still new to your shape and what this all means. I wouldn't, I mean, *we* wouldn't risk your life this way."

Diwata snorted. Magnús ignored her.

"But maybe if I fly at them, I can do something. Remember that I didn't die before. If I'm a demigod like Diwata says, maybe—"

"It's too risky, Altair," Magnús said firmly, taking the human's hands. "We don't know the extent of your powers or of your protections. Trolls are very dangerous, and this is not the time or place to test them." He wanted to hug Altair, to kiss him, to banish his worry. He shouldn't.

«You should,» Ólafur said in his mind.

«Shut up, Cousin. Worry about your own love life.»

«Hah! You admit you think about love when you think about Altair.»

Magnús was sorely tempted to close his mind firmly to Ólafur's , but he recognized the undertone of nerves. Magnús at least had experience fighting trolls; Ólafur had none. Even an invisible reconnaissance mission into a troll nest must be terrifying, but his cousin was willing to risk it to help Magnús's friend.

«Fine, you win. I have feelings for him,» Magnús thought back instead of making light.

«Tell him. There are no guarantees for any of us. You in particular, given the prophecy.»

When they had finally been able to explain to Altair what was going on, the human's eyes had grown wider and wider as they told him about the prophecy and the various attacks they had undergone. Magnús had rushed over the part about his own doom if Altair lived, but he had seen anguish in the young man's face.

"Diwata, may we have a moment alone?" Magnús asked. She nodded and stepped a few paces away.

Holding Altair's hands tightly, Magnús leaned close. "Whether we triumph or fail this night, Altair Fálkason, I want you to know this. You have come to mean much to me in the scant days we have spent together. Your wit, your humor, your excitement for life...I treasure them. I understand that you have no great love for this country, and I can't blame you. Before you leave our shores, though, I long for time together where I can know you better without these shards of prophecy hanging over us."

Altair's eyes shimmered in the near-black night, a sheen of gold that hadn't been there before his transformation. It was the Falcon emerging, Magnús thought, and the sweep of pride that brought to him—the realization that this remarkable human was even more special than Magnús had come to know—took his breath away.

"I-I really like you," Altair blurted out. "I know that's crazy. I only just met you, but I had to... I wanted to say..." He bit his lower lip and fell silent.

Magnús could no longer resist. He pulled Altair close and bent to hug him, allowing the miracle of this young man in his arms to take him completely. Altair returned the embrace a bit awkwardly, as if he were inexperienced. Perhaps he was, but he caught on quickly. Altair wrapped his arms tightly around Magnús, and there was more strength there than Magnús would have expected.

Altair leaned away but didn't let go. He looked up at Magnús, his golden eyes gleaming more brightly. "Be safe, Magnús. Take no risks. Please. I know your friend is important to you, but I couldn't bear it if anything happened to you."

"I'll be safe," Magnús promised, though he knew it was something of a lie. He wasn't getting out of this adventure alive. If the trolls didn't get him, something else ugly awaited down future's path. But he would face it gladly for the chance to keep Altair safe.

He couldn't say any of that out loud, so instead he hugged Altair again, then stepped back.

"Ready?" he called softly to Diwata, then thought the same to Ólafur. They answered yes. "Then here we go."

FOURTEEN

A visible Magnús approached the cave opening, casually tossing a glowing blue stone in the air as he strode across the sand. Two trolls lumbered out of the cave opening. A piece of leather, fastened tightly around the upper arm of each, was embossed with a rune Magnús had come to know well.

The behemoths stopped side by side after a few feet. Not distant enough from the opening for Ólafur's safety yet, as they knew of at least one more troll.

"Greetings from Grýla Trollmother," Magnús called cheerfully, hoping the name would give them pause.

Instead, the trolls looked at each other and grinned. Their rocky teeth were jagged and broken.

"Hear him, Skyrgámur," said one of the trolls. "Mother sends greetings." As it spoke, it pulled an enormous meat hook from behind its back.

"Curious, Ketkrókur, since she isn't speaking to us," answered the other, bringing forth a wooden cudgel.

Magnús's heart sank. Bad enough the trolls were smart enough to talk, but worse because he knew those names. Ketkrókur and

Skyrgámur were two of the Jólasveinar. The Yule Lads. And where two were found, quite possibly the other eleven might be as well.

«Careful, Óli. It's Grýla's children, maybe more than these two.»

As if summoned, a third troll emerged from the cave. This one was oddly stiff and walked with a side-to-side gait. It was the Yule Lad called Stekkjarstaur, if Magnús had to guess, based on its peg legs.

"Did Mother send us a snack?" he asked his brother trolls.

"More than one," Ketkrókur said, pointing to Diwata with his hook.

"Just try to eat me," Diwata shouted.

Magnús hurled one of his stones at Skyrgámur and skipped back. The beast raised its cudgel and came after Magnús, as he'd hoped.

The other two went for Diwata. She threw a piece of wood down in their path and shouted words Magnús didn't recognize but thought were from giantish. The wood lengthened and thickened, becoming a large...worm? Or more like a snake.

The transfigured wood reared its front half off the ground, then struck at the trolls. They yelped and dodged, swinging their weapons. The snake managed to knock Stekkjarstaur off his stiff legs, then turned to its brother.

Magnús gave his attention to the troll trying to catch him, leaping back and out of its clumsy reach. Together, he and Diwata had managed to draw the three away from the cave opening.

«I'm going in,» Ólafur said.

Magnús hurled another stone at his foe and one at Ketkrókur, who was trying to get at Diwata around her snake. The troll grunted and changed direction, coming after Magnús instead. Diwata darted after it, slamming it on the back with another of her staves.

"Stay still," she cried, and the troll came to a halt, frozen in the moment of taking a step. "Obedience spell," she called to Magnús. "I don't know how long it will last."

Her snake had coiled around Stekkjarstaur. The troll was gripping its head, trying to choke it but apparently without effect. This was going better than Magnús had hoped. Two trolls down already.

As if on cue, Ólafur groaned mentally. «Oh shit. Incoming.»

At the same time, Altair yelled, "Magnús! Look out, on your left."

He whirled in time to see a creature leaping straight at him. It was the size of a huge dog, with ears like a fox, glowing red eyes, and slavering fangs. The claws at the end of its paws were hooked like a cat's and seemed very sharp. Magnús ducked, but the creature snagged its claws into Magnús's shirt and pulled him down on top of it.

Dimly, he was aware of shapes emerging from the cave mouth as well. As he held off the fox-cat's jaws with both hands, he risked a glance. The things coming out of the cave were lumpy, seemed awkward on their webbed feet, and glowed greenish in the dim light. They were bigger than huldufólk, but not as big or rocky as trolls.

"Hafmenn!" he called to warn the others. "Mermen."

The beast struggling with him scratched deeply with its claws, drawing silvery blood from Magnús. He heard Diwata scream, and then a thud. He couldn't take his eyes off the fox-cat going for his throat, though. Somewhere, he heard Altair shout, though it sounded more angry than hurt. A whoosh of wings, and suddenly the fox-cat was dragged off of him. A huge golden falcon had the creature in its talons.

«Altair,» Magnús thought at him with deep fondness. «I told you to stay back.»

«No fucking way am I letting this thing hurt you.»

The words came with a fierce, possessive pride that Magnús

found he liked. The falcon swiftly winged over the waves, the beast writhing helplessly in his talons, until Altair dropped it. It screeched horribly as it fell, something between a yowl and a bark. Then it hit the water hard.

Magnús looked around. Two of the Yule Lads were flanking Diwata, though they couldn't seem to get at her through a shimmer that arose from one of her staves. Diwata's hands flung wide, and she worked up the spell for a blizzard like she had used before. The waves crashing against the rocks increased their intensity, and the night air turned icy.

A screech made him whirl away from Diwata. A hafmaður was casting spears up at Altair, who was trying to dive into attack with his talons. The third Yule Lad pulled a thick net from somewhere and spread it, ready to throw at Altair if he got low enough.

«Back away, Altair! There are too many.»

As if to prove Magnús's point, he was knocked to the ground. Rolling over and up into a defensive position, he snarled at the hafmaður, its sickly green glow burning brighter in the sharp tips of its webbed hands. As with the trolls, it bore a badge carrying the runic symbol of this... what? Cult? Army?

The sea creature fell on him with a disgustingly damp stench like rotting seaweed and tried to choke him. It might have succeeded, but something whacked it on the back of its head, and it fell off Magnús. He looked up into the grim, blood-streaked face of Karl, holding a thick piece of driftwood.

"Thank the gods," Magnús murmured, both at the assistance and that Karl was alive.

"Thank your cousin. He let me and the others out. But he's in trouble." Karl turned to run back down the beach, to where Ólafur was surrounded by three of the mermen. Ólafur was wide eyed and looked panicky, though he was keeping the hafmenn at bay with his knife.

Karl dove at one of the mermen and pulled it to the ground.

Thick flakes of snow filled the air, and an ice-laden gust of wind slammed into another of the mermen. Magnús pulled out Sæmundur's dagger as he reached the fight. He sliced across the back of the third merman, leaving a streak of silver fire and a smell of burning seaweed. It made a ghastly noise as it scrambled away toward the water.

The growing snowstorm abruptly died away, and Ólafur shouted, "Dee!"

The witch had been unable to keep the Yule Lads at bay. One held her off the ground by her shirt, and her head lolled; whether she was dead or unconscious, Magnús couldn't tell. Ólafur and Karl both charged toward the trolls.

Magnús started after them, but the third Yule Lad grabbed him from behind, then threw him to the hard sand. He dropped the enchanted dagger, grunting in pain. The troll placed its broad foot on his back and pressed Magnús into the ground.

A thrumming sound filled the air then, a deep throb coming from somewhere. It was growing closer, he thought, as he fought to keep the troll from crushing his ribs.

Ketkrókur seemed not to hear the pulsation. It merely chuckled behind Magnús.

"Fine meat for the stewpot tonight. Let's see if we've learned to cook at Grýla's hearth."

As Magnús struggled, he was aware of more mermen emerging from the sea. They were being overwhelmed. Where was Altair? Was he safe?

And what in the Nine Worlds was that *beating* sound? It was too strong for seagulls, even louder than Altair's wings. Sand and ice blew around the beach, driven in a gale that came from over the mountain.

At that moment, Ketkrókur reached down to grab Magnús by the arm. The troll pulled so hard that Magnús felt the shoulder dislocate. The already dark world grayed out even more, and he nearly passed out from pain. What kept him conscious was the need to know: what was that sound, and where was his Falcon?

«Altair! Get away!»

A screech as loud as thunder, as sharp as glass, broke over the beach. A vast shadow blocked what little light they had. Ketkrókur was knocked away from Magnús with a brush of wings that, as they passed over the elf's body, felt like steel more than feathers.

Magnús writhed onto his back, clutching his shoulder, looking up in awe. An enormous eagle, wingspan twice as wide as Altair's, swept over the battle. With the eagle were hundreds of other birds. They dove and pecked at the mermen, driving them away and back into the water.

The massive raptor clutched at the troll menacing Ólafur and Karl, flinging it dozens of yards to smash against a rock cliff. Ólafur and Karl went after the troll that had Diwata and, between the two of them, managed to make it drop the witch. Altair joined that fight in his falcon shape, swiping viciously as he made passes, until the Yule Lad turned and ran.

In what seemed like no time, the whirlwind of birds and sand and feathers died down. Panting, Magnús stood up awkwardly, hand to his painful shoulder, to look around.

The battle was over. Even in the pitch-black night, a radiance had stolen over the sand. The Yule Lads were down or had run away. Bodies of dead hafmenn lay on the sand. Three humans Magnús didn't know, each clutching some kind of makeshift weapon, blinked around them uncertainly. Ólafur was on his knees, cradling Diwata, but she was already stirring.

Karl dropped his club and walked over to the three unknown humans; he seemed to be trying to explain to them what was going on. Perhaps they'd been prisoners with Karl.

And Altair? Magnús scanned the sky and saw the Falcon

descending toward him. As it touched the beach, it became a naked human, concern on his face.

"Are you all right?" Altair demanded, running his hands lightly over Magnús's body.

"My shoulder," Magnús groaned. "I just need to..." He gritted his teeth and shoved his shoulder back into place, then fell to his knees from the white-hot flare of pain.

«—Altair Fálkason—»

The voice that throbbed and rumbled across the beach made everyone turn to look. The huge Eagle had perched on a column of basalt, Their wings spread wide. Despite the hour of night, They glowed white against the black ocean. They were the source of the radiance illuminating the remnants of battle.

A gust of wind swept past the Eagle and over the fighters, carrying to them the most delicious smell of clean winds and snow. The freshening breeze soothed Magnús's pained shoulder. At a small distance, Diwata sat up, looking fully recovered, as did the others. Altair fell to his knees, awe and wonder on his face.

Then Magnús finally understood what was happening, and he, too, went to his knees, to honor and thank Gammur the Eagle, mighty Landvættur of the North.

CHAPTER
FIFTEEN

Altair gazed in wonder at the white Eagle, alit on an outcropping of rock, talons wrapped around a basalt spar. Their wings spread wide, to a span of more than forty feet, as They raised Their beak and called to the encircling birds, in words Altair felt more than heard:

«—Rejoice, ye brethren of the sky. Rejoice! The herald of Gammur
has returned.—»

Caws and cries and gentle coos filled the air, bringing tears to Altair's eyes. So much joy there, such welcome. Could it really be for him?

Magnús and Ólafur were already on their knees, and Altair saw Diwata bow. Belatedly, Altair realized he was just staring, so he lowered his head awkwardly as well. But he couldn't look away for long. He hungered f0r the sight of the glorious raptor that had come to save them, and more tears formed at Their beauty and majesty.

Gammur beat Their wings before lowering Their enormous

head to meet Altair's gaze. "Thou art Duke of the Winds and need never bow to me," Gammur said.

The voice was the kind, warm one Altair had heard in his head when he first transformed, but he understood it like the bird calls around him.

Altair heard Ólafur whisper to Magnús, "I don't know what they're saying."

"My apologies, ye huldufólk and loyal witch," Gammur said in Icelandic. "I am overcome with joy to welcome the son of my faithful herald. Far from this place of power, Fálki ventured on dire quest, though it broke the hearts of us both to be separated. The winds have not been as fierce or as sustaining these last centuries without my Falcon to bring me tidings."

"You knew my father?" Altair was surprised at the sudden flash of anger in his own voice. "And you call him loyal?" Then, again mindful that this Eagle was something between a king and a god, he added belatedly, "My lord."

"Aye, knew Fálki Veðurfölnisson and loved him. True as the North Wind, strong as the gale, was my Falcon for many hundreds of years. He would not have left this land excepting great need and services to the Landvættir."

"Are you sure we're talking about the same person?" Altair demanded. "My father abandoned my mother and me when I was little. I don't think he was loyal or strong."

The Eagle rustled Their wings, golden beak flashing in the sunlight. "Once Fálki left these shores, I could no longer see him or protect him, but I felt his joy when his heir was born more than twenty years ago, and I felt his agony when he died three years later. The Fálki I knew would not have abandoned his child and heir."

"Well, that can't be right," Altair argued. "My dad only died a few years ago."

"How do you know that?" Magnús asked gently. He had edged closer, so quietly that Altair didn't even feel him approach.

"My uncle told me so," Altair answered stubbornly. "Dad had another family after he left us, and he lived with them until he had a heart attack. My uncle finally found out about me and came looking, but it was too late. By then, my mother had already died too."

"Fálki had no brother," Gammur said. "He was the unique fledgling of the prior Falcon, as thou art the unique fledgling of Fálki. It is the way of things, set down long, long ago."

"Mighty Eagle," Magnús began, gazing reverently up at Gammur. "If it would please you to tell Altair how came his father to leave Iceland, perhaps some mysteries may be answered."

The Eagle lowered Their head on Their long neck and shifted Their perch on the outcropping. "Wise art thou becoming, Magnús Bryndísarson, and correct, to point out that even the great can be careless. Very well. Altair Fálkason, I ask thee to accompany me a short way. These matters are for the ears of naught but the Landvættir and their most intimate allies."

With that, the Eagle launched into the dark skies with a downbeat of Their wings. In seconds, They were hundreds of feet above the ground and climbing higher still.

"Move it, bird boy," Diwata hissed when Altair hesitated. "Transform and go follow the big guy. We're out of time."

Not really believing everything that had happened in the past days—and that continued to happen—Altair let the transformation come over him once more. He was in the air a moment later, slipping into an updraft as he soared after Gammur. A faint hint of dawn had begun to lighten the horizon, and Altair could sense it would be a beautiful, clear morning.

In Falcon form, he felt the irresistible pull of the Eagle. Although the white figure was a mile above him at least, his eyes would not look away from the glory of the Landvættur. With powerful beats of his wings, finding updrafts by instinct, he was soon flying and wheeling near to Gammur.

"My heart is full," the Eagle called to him, again in Their own language that no human or elf would be able to understand. "Long have I missed the companionship of my herald, who was more than servant and far more than friend."

"Then why did he have to leave Iceland?" Altair asked.

"A human steeped in the ways of dark sorcery and of traffic with horrible powers had devised a spell powerful enough to enslave even the Landvættir," Gammur said. "This sorcerer kept knowledge of the spell so hidden that no word of it reached even my Falcon at the time. Fortunately, this magician, a bishop who called himself Gottskálk, died before he could attempt the spell on my brethren or on me."

"Gottskálk!" Altair cried out, the sharp call of a falcon startled into flight. "The draugur I met. He wrote the, the, um, book of bad spells, didn't he?"

"Aye, Rauðskinna is what the humans called his horrific galdrabók of dark magic. But we Landvættir knew aught of his accomplishments at the time. It was many, many years later that another sorcerer attempted to wrest possession of the Rauðskinna from the dead bishop.

"This time word reached us, of a magician who called himself Galdra-Loftur, as steeped in darkness as Gottskálk. He had discovered the secrets of immortality but wanted still more. He had visions of summoning and imprisoning the fire giant Surtur whom humans, in that faith they call Christianity, termed Satan, the father of evil."

"Surtur? He rules Muspellsheimur, I think Bryndís said."

"Correct, fledgling. His power is near as great as the Æsir, and yet this Galdra-Loftur believed he could capture Surtur and enslave him."

"Using the spell in the Rauðskinna." Some things were becoming clearer to him.

"Aye. Thy father became aware of Galdra-Loftur and his delusions and so tracked his movements. Fálki was there in Hólar when the sorcerer and a circle of his acolytes worked horrible spells to bring the ghost of Gottskálk back from the plains of Hel. They tortured the spirit to force it to reveal the location of the Rauðskinna, which he had buried and concealed before his death."

"I met Gottskálk's ghost. Underneath where the school at Hólar was."

"An evil man punished by a greater evil and then denied his rest." Gammur shivered Their wings in flight. "In that time, loyal Fálki heard the shrieks of Gottskalk's spirit and conceived the idea that a spell powerful enough to bind Surtur could be a threat to his beloved Gammur as well. And so he flew, swift as thought, to the revealed location. Before Galdra-Loftur could arrive, my Falcon found the accursed book and brought it to me."

Altair banked and flew higher, soaring over the vast sea as the first rays of dawn colored the waves. His father, taking such risks, confronting the same evils Altair had encountered... He didn't know how to get a grip on the idea.

Gammur rose near Altair on powerful beats of Their white wings. "I heard his fears and risked myself to look into the Rauðskinna. Fálki was correct. The spell could bind even the most powerful magical spirits in Iceland.

"In the meantime, though denied the spell he wanted, Galdra-Loftur made his attempt to enslave Surtur. The attempt failed, and Galdra-Loftur vanished. The Landvættir convened in secret, and we agreed that the binding spell could not be allowed to fall into the hands of Galdra-Loftur, if he lived, or any other black sorcerer."

The voice of the Eagle grew sad, poignant enough to break

Altair's heart. "My loyal, brave, beloved Fálki took the solution upon himself. He left Iceland with the Rauðskinna, almost three hundred years ago. He vowed—for love of me and of this land— never to return.

"And thereafter, as I said, I could touch his mind no longer. Only the most powerful emotions could reach me, like the love he found with thy mother, his joy in thy birth, and the agony and despair of his death."

A host of raw emotions washed through Altair, battering his mind and heart. For almost twenty years, he'd believed his father had abandoned his family. Abandoned his son. To hear that Fálki's joy had been so great at Altair's birth that Gammur could feel it thousands of miles away... Had Fálki actually been killed, and that was why he disappeared? He hadn't abandoned Altair at all, but was taken from his family.

Then what did that mean about Uncle Trausti? Why would he lie about Fálki's supposed second family and recent death?

"Ah, Fálki, would that thee had returned to these shores," Gammur called to the winds. "While the Eagle lives, the Falcon cannot die. We are one, you see? I am the Guardian of the North, but no matter how high I fly, how far I see, still I am constrained to guard this portion of Iceland. I need the Falcon to bring me tidings and warnings."

The Eagle rose even higher, far above the clouds now, dawn's rays limning Their white wings in gold. "Altair Fálkason, wilt thou take up the mantle of thine father and his father before him? Wilt thou bind thyself to the Landvættir and to this mighty work? Wilt thou keep sharp watch, and bring me word of joy and threat alike? Wilt thou live while the Eagle lives, soar through the icy air, carry on my task if I should fall? Wilt thou take thy appointed place, in Fálki's stead, as my Falcon?"

Altair's easy flight faltered for a moment. He suddenly felt like a human again, an orphan. He lived in Boston, not Iceland. He was a graduate student, not a mystical spirit or demigod.

Gammur's resonant cry recalled him to the winds. He twisted the tips of his wings and caught an updraft. Again he soared, miles above the fjords and the sea, the gray and green landscape sweeping across his vision as he wheeled. His eyesight was so sharp that he could see the camper van in which he and his friends had crossed Iceland. Could see Diwata and Ólafur engaged in conversation with Karl and the other humans they had rescued. Could see Magnús scanning the sky for him, one hand shading his eyes from the rising sun, his silver-blond hair streaming in the breeze off the fjord where it had come loose from its bun. Magnús with his grace and his magic and his passion to protect the humans of Iceland.

Who was Altair? He was meek, gawky, too young, too intense, not someone who could hold the interest or attention of a man like Magnús.

"I don't know if I can stay here," he answered Gammur, aware as he did so of the protest in his soul. "I don't belong. I, I need some time. Please."

The screech of the Landvættur known as the Eagle was heartbreaking, but Gammur did not try to sway Altair. The two mighty birds flew in silence a little longer. Twice, Altair nearly cried out that he'd decided, that he wanted to stay. The story of his father moved him in ways he couldn't process.

He found it impossible to doubt the Eagle, though. Just like with Magnús, Altair trusted Gammur immediately and completely. He wanted to be worthy of the sacrifice his father had made.

But he couldn't say it. Even with all the uncertainties about his uncle and with Willa and Jason, he wasn't sure if he could give up the only life he knew in Boston for one of mystery and magic in Iceland.

The Eagle spiraled downward, and Altair followed. When Gammur landed on Their rocky perch again, talons curled around the basalt ledge, Altair alit next to Magnús. Effortlessly, he shifted back to human and then shivered in the cold. Magnús didn't say a word but adjusted his stance to shield Altair from the view of the others.

"I left my clothes up there," Altair said, gesturing to the hill fifteen or twenty yards away from the beach. Magnús nodded and moved with him as he went to retrieve them.

He climbed a hillock covered in yellow grasses, to where he had set aside his satchel and stripped off his clothes shamelessly when Magnús went down under that hideous dog-like thing. Altair was sure he had left them on this spot where bare rock showed through the grass, but now he saw no sign of them.

No, wait, his pants were over there, with a shoe, farther away from the group on the beach. He hurried over to pick them up and spotted his sweater caught on a clump of some spiky plant he didn't know, down in a dell between two hillocks.

Magnús had followed. "What is this? Why are your clothes all over?"

"I don't know," Altair answered as he fumbled with what he could find. No underwear to be seen, but he didn't want his bare butt flashing the crowd. "And I don't see my satchel anywhere. Was someone else here while I flew with Gammur?"

"I didn't see anyone. I was focused on watching you fly. You're glorious, Altair."

Altair blushed, hiding his burning cheeks with the sweater he pulled over his head. He tugged it into place to keep his hands busy and looked at a clump of small, purple flowers. Quietly, he said, "Gammur asked me to stay in Iceland."

A sharp inhalation made him look up. The expression on Magnús's face was... Altair didn't know what to think. Magnús's blue eyes seemed especially bright, his expressive mouth moved between a smile and a frown, and Altair would have said his posture was hesitant and yet excited. Hopeful, yet guarded.

"What did you answer?" Magnús asked, his deep voice sounding tense, even anxious.

Did Magnús feel the same way that Altair did? He had said Altair meant something to him, but was it anything like Altair's growing certainty that he was in love with Magnús?

"Um, I, I told Gammur I wasn't sure. That I should stay, I mean."

Magnús turned his face away, but not before Altair registered a fleeting glimpse of sadness, of grief. Maybe it was at the thought of Altair leaving. But more likely, Magnús was thinking of the land wights, which he clearly revered. He was thinking of Iceland, and how important the Landvættir were to protection. Magnús would have never turned down the honor of serving the Eagle, Altair was sure.

"I don't know how I can be needed," Altair stumbled to explain. "I'm an American from Boston. I don't know anything about magical threats. There must be someone from Iceland who would do a better job."

Magnús wouldn't look at him, but when he answered, his voice was low and sad. "I think I understand. You have had one terrifying adventure and encounter after the other since we met. I have not been able to keep you safe. Why would you want to stay in a country that endangers you so?"

I would stay for you, Altair wanted to say. But that was ridiculous, wasn't it? He was a mortal, with a tiny lifespan compared to Magnús's. In what world would Magnús ever want to be with a human like Altair?

Though he wasn't just human, not anymore. He was the Falcon, and Gammur had said something about him not being able to die while the Eagle lived. His own father had left Iceland hundreds of years before. Did that all mean Altair would live, well, if not forever, then long enough that a life with Magnús was possible?

"Magnús, I want—"

"I see another shoe, over there," Magnús said, his voice slightly hoarse.

Altair picked it up and sat to pull on the rest of his recovered clothes. "But what happened to my satchel?" he said. "And how did my stuff get so scattered?"

"Maybe it was the beating of your wings when you transformed," Magnús said dully. "Let's go back. Your bag may have gotten blown in a different direction."

Suddenly, a thought popped into Altair's head. Yes, he was sure. "It's through that, uh, kind of valley over there, and up that rock on top."

Magnús looked back at him, puzzled. "What makes you think that?"

"I don't know. But I'm positive. Maybe I spotted it subconsciously as I was coming down to land."

Altair hurried forward, feeling the certainty grow. Yes, the bag was just through this meadow, up this rock that had cracked to form something akin to stairs. He moved faster, almost slipping on the rough stone.

Dimly, he was aware of Magnús behind him, calling his name, telling him to wait. But he couldn't wait. He wanted his satchel, and it was this way. Magnús could catch up to him.

He reached the top of the rough stairs and found himself at the edge of a flat expanse of lichen-covered rock. Its gray and green surface was uneven and broken, forming a plain as wide as a football field. He hurried forward because, yes, there it was. His bag was lying on the ground. Never mind that they were now hundreds of yards from where he'd transformed.

Magnús called out behind him, "Wait! Something is very wrong here!"

Altair reached for his satchel, dismayed to discover it had been ripped open. His notes, his laptop—they were there but mangled, as if something large had gripped the bag.

He looked at the broken contents, grief-stricken. All his work. His research. And...and... wasn't there something else, too? Something missing?

Magnús reached him and inhaled sharply when he saw the ripped-open satchel. "Transform. Now!"

Something whistled through the air, and Magnús was knocked off his feet. He flew backwards a few yards, hitting the ground hard. Something else kicked Altair's feet out from under him. His ass hit the rock painfully.

Groaning, he looked up at a shimmer that towered above him, the same shimmer Altair could see when Magnús didn't try hard enough to be invisible.

"Huldufólk!" Altair shouted, to warn Magnús.

A chuckle sounded from thin air, and a male elf suddenly became visible. His hair was similar to Magnús's, though a shade darker, yet his gray eyes showed none of Magnús's warmth. With a gesture of his hand, two large trolls also could be seen, one standing with its boulder-like foot on Magnús's chest.

The elf looming over Altair smiled broadly and said, "Greetings, Falcon. We haven't been introduced, but I'm sure that one" —he gestured at Magnús—"would have told you about me. I am Lars Berkisson, sometimes known as the Black Priest."

Magnús roared out his fury, hatred thick in his voice. The troll holding him down applied more pressure, and Magnús groaned.

Lars ignored him and held aloft a book. It was Altair's grandmother's diary, he realized. And then realized that he had forgotten he had it with him. How was that possible?"

"I thank you for bringing me this," Lars continued. "Now we can begin."

CHAPTER

SIXTEEN

Magnús pushed his hands uselessly against the crushing weight of the troll's foot that kept him pinned to the ground. His ribs felt like they were breaking under the pressure, but he could get no leverage. He tried to reach Ólafur's mind, to warn him or to ask for help, but he couldn't feel his cousin.

Had the rest of the group been attacked as well? There must be a spell that could help him get loose, but his rage at Lars, at the ambush, was overwhelming.

And there the bastard stood, free, alive, looming over Altair. Had Lars done that to Sigurjón, too? Had he revealed himself after he tricked Sigurjón into the fall?

"You son of a bitch," he groaned. "Get away from Altair."

Lars didn't even look up from the book in his hands, but he laughed. "I'm afraid another of your pets is going to be lost to you, Cousin. You should have learned your lesson with the first one and stayed away."

That book... Magnús suddenly realized he had known about

115

the book, had seen it in Altair's possession. But somehow, he had just forgotten about it. Ignored it. "What is that thing?" he hissed.

Finally, Lars deigned to meet Magnús's eyes. His lips curved into a cruel grin as he held up the small book, perhaps seven inches tall and bound in a garish pink, floral cover. "This? Nothing important, nothing anyone would notice or remember seeing. We made sure."

Altair gasped. "That's my grandmother's diary. Nobody would care about that. I remember putting it away in Boston, but I haven't thought about it since."

Lars held the book up by the edges of its covers, pages open toward him, and said a word in a language Magnús didn't recognize. On the pink cover, an image flared to life briefly, white fire flickering for a moment before fading.

"A rune," Magnús said. "You hid it behind a rune."

Lars laughed. "Oh, this is only the first level of protection. A galdur of forgetting. Remarkably effective, and simple to achieve with the right training."

He tsked reprovingly. "We intended it just for the Falcon, but it affected you, too, Magnús Bryndísarson. For shame. No huldufólk should be so easily manipulated. But then, you align yourself closely with the invading vermin."

He stroked a finger down the rune and suddenly, Magnús recalled seeing the book before. *Several* times. He'd looked in Altair's satchel once while escorting Altair to the university, seen the book, and then forgotten it ever happened. Pursued by the draugur in Hólar, *all* of them had seen the book when they'd been chased into the room with Sæmundur's relics and then forgotten it. Other moments, too, that had simply been erased.

Magnús cursed himself for a fool. Even though he'd known something like that was happening to Altair, it had never occurred to him that he might be snared as well.

Lars said a second word and another rune flashed, this one

violet. "Compulsion," he explained. "To keep the book safe and hidden at all times. Very effective in getting this treasure safely into my hands."

To the trolls, Lars called out in their tongue, "Bring the human and the elf to the altar. Gammur will be here soon, and I must complete the preparations."

Magnús struggled again to free himself as the troll that had held him down grabbed his hair and his arm. It had a symbol in red paint on one of its arms, the same one Magnús had found taunting him around Iceland, even on Altair's neck. The rune stood out sharply against the troll's rocky gray skin as it dragged Magnús effortlessly across the field.

Altair batted feebly at the grip of the second troll. It also bore the rune in red. Both creatures stopped about ten yards behind Lars, who faced away from them, book in one hand and a thick stylus in the other.

The trolls threw Magnús and Altair to the ground, then crouched gracelessly to pin their shoulders down. When they ceased moving, they resembled rocky outcroppings, the kind that dotted the landscape of Iceland.

Lars walked forward and climbed something that wasn't there.

"An illusion," Magnús spat out. "That's Lars's special gift, to create illusions," he called to Altair, hatred making him nearly choke. "It's how he killed Sigurjón, too. What *is* that book?"

Altair exhaled roughly. "I have a bad feeling. Gammur told me about a very dangerous book of magic spells, the same one Diwata mentioned."

Magnús gaped at him. "You don't mean... That couldn't be the Rauðskinna."

Apparently standing two yards off the ground on nothing, Lars gestured abruptly with the dowel in his hand. His illusion fell away, revealing a squarish stone platform, about fifteen yards to a side, with stairs leading up on each side. In the center of the platform were two stone columns, about seven or eight yards apart.

Altair groaned. "I don't like the look of that thing at all."

Magnús had to agree. It resembled nothing so much as an altar.

Lars went to one knee, consulting the book in hand as he sketched on the surface of the platform with the dowel. Words were tumbling from his mouth, too, and pressure built in the air. The sky, which had begun to lighten with dawn, darkened again as black storm clouds gathered unnaturally fast.

Magnús could feel it. Something very, very powerful was being wrought, and he instinctively dreaded it.

Winds gusted, then blew more strongly, bringing the scent of the ocean spray with them. Another sense of throbbing began, but from a different direction.

Altair's face lit up. "It's Gammur! I can feel Them. They're coming!"

Lars must have heard Altair, but he continued to make his marks on the ground, seemingly unperturbed. Magnús could hear the beat of powerful wings, sense the changing pressure in the air as the mighty Eagle drew closer.

"He has the Rauðskinna!" Altair shouted to alert Gammur. "I can't change shape."

"Huldumaður, what art thee playing at?" Gammur roared as They flew into sight, wheeling above the clearing. "I see it now. The book in thine hand was already the greatest evil conceived in this Realm, and thou hast made it even more of an abomination. Alas, for my poor Fálki. And thee, Lars Berkisson? Hast thou aligned thyself against thy native land, the home set aside for thee and thy kin by the gods themselves?"

Lars stood straight again and looked up at the Eagle. "The Æsir betrayed this land by allowing humans to come here. We will set things right and restore our home to the haven it was always meant to be!"

With that, he pointed up at Gammur with the dowel and cried out three words. Lightning split the sky, striking rocky plinths and grass hillocks on all sides. The Eagle screeched but pivoted, easily avoiding the bolts. On the stone slab, the pillars had turned black as pitch.

Lars gestured again with the dowel in a dramatic ground-ward motion. Gammur's flight stuttered as a powerful downdraft roared at Them, bending the grass in swirling ways and scouring the area clear of rubble. The Eagle regained Their mastery of the air, but the gust had brought Them closer to the ground.

With a triumphant cry, Lars made a gesture with both book and dowel. The blackness that had appeared on the pillars surged upward like oil or pitch, somehow oozing into the air with tremendous speed. The shadows wrapped around the Eagle's wings and dragged Them down to the ground. Another shadow clamped the Eagle's beak shut. They struggled and used Their talons, until more shadows oozed from the pillars and encased those as well.

Trapped, the great Landvættur, mighty Gammur, was held fast between the pillars, wings outstretched, head and feet swathed in something that resembled liquid obsidian.

"The last spell of Bishop Gottskálk Nikulásson," Lars said in a voice dripping with satisfaction and glee. "Shackles powerful enough to hold even one of the Landvættir."

"Let Them go," Altair screamed, writhing and pushing against the troll that held him down.

"This is the greatest sacrilege imaginable," Magnús shouted. "The queen will have your life for this."

Lars laughed bitterly. "Hildur can have my life if she can reach me. But she is about to learn the consequences of banishing me to

Miðgarður. The trickle of magic that enters those lands is both feeble and nauseating.

"For years I wandered in that miserable human cesspool, hating every smell, every taste, every sight. Until one day I stumbled across the Black School. There I learned the error of my approach, as well as the solution. With training and patience, I made the sacrifice. I learned the magic of the galdur, that sorcery peculiar to humans. When the master of the school saw my loyalty and my commitment, he showed me how Iceland could be saved."

"You will bring death upon Iceland," Magnús said venomously. "The Nornir have warned us. This path will bring destruction to all."

"Lies! This is the way to scour Iceland of the infection of humans. With their joyless buildings and their corrupted politicians and their shameless abuse of the natural wonders of this country. We will use their own magics and their deepest fears to drive the foreign invaders away forever, put the mundane humans back in their proper place as servants, muzzle the witches, and remake this country into the paradise the gods once intended before they betrayed us."

"Madness. You are insane."

"I am enlightened, Cousin," Lars said, again brandishing the book. "The master of my school had learned where the Falcon hid this when he left Iceland. With my gifts, though weakened in Miðgarður, it was easy to lure Fálki away to an isolated place and let my master take his revenge. It transpired that the Falcon's immortality only protects him within the reach of Iceland."

"My father," Altair cried, aghast. "He didn't leave us. You murdered him."

"Yet we brought him back to Iceland, in a fashion," Lars said. He mouthed another word and a third rune glowed on the pink covers of the book. The floral fabric faded away, revealing a mottled, tanned surface beneath. It looked horribly like—

Altair sobbed. "You skinned him. You skinned my father and covered that book with him."

"Gruesome but effective. Concealing the Rauðskinna in the Falcon's skin and arranging to have it always in your company, little godling, confused the senses of the Landvættir. They could not feel the true nature of the galdrabók beneath its new binding."

This was what the ghost of Gottskálk had sensed, Magnús realized suddenly. The dead bishop had known they carried his Rauðskinna. If he had just realized...

No. Self-recriminations could wait.

"And so you have trapped the Eagle in the Bishop's Shackles," Magnús seethed instead, his jaw clenched. "There are still three more Landvættir, and all the forces of the huldufólk will be arrayed against you."

"While I have most of the trolls and many, *many* of the inhabitants of Iceland who hate the human invasion as much as I. And more besides. I will do what no invader ever managed. While the Eagle lies trapped, I will bring a great sorcerer here who will help me restore Iceland to its rightful owners."

Lars thrust both arms into the air and shouted another spell into the wind. The clouds darkened even more and grew ponderous, seeming to swell toward the altar. The trapped Eagle struggled frantically but to no avail. The winds whistled to a high pitch, swirling around the clearing, sweeping up debris and rubble.

A thin whirlwind extended from the lowest of the storm clouds, stretching downward. Lars chanted, manic glee on his face as his clothes whipped around him in the gale. Magnús had to narrow his eyes against the fierce wind; if the trolls hadn't held him down, he would have been swept away.

With the sound of a freight train roaring by, the whirlwind touched the ground just beside Gammur and then vanished. In its place was a man, a tall figure in black, his shoulders wide, his face partially hidden by a broad hat brim.

Magnús knew this man's shape from the horrible prophecies of Diwata. He wanted to weep. Everything she foresaw was coming true—the Falcon had led Magnús to the Black Priest and unwittingly brought to him the Bishop's Shackles. Now here was the sorcerer who would kill Altair and destroy Iceland if Magnús couldn't stop him.

Beside Magnús, Altair had stopped struggling. When Magnús glanced at him, the young man's mouth was gaping, horror spread across his features.

"Uncle Trausti?" Altair asked, sounding like he was in shock.

"Greetings, Nephew," the sorcerer said, a wide grin giving him the look of a deranged man. "Well, perhaps not 'Nephew.' But I enjoyed very much getting to use you to undo the bad turn your father Fálki delivered unto me. Putting the Rauðskinna in your hands, telling you a story about it being your grandmother's diary...delightful."

He swept grandly as if in a bow, but when he straightened up again, a dagger with a black blade was in his right hand. Dark flames danced along the weapon's edge.

"I am Galdra-Loftur Þorsteinsson. Four hundred years I have studied and waited to accomplish my vision. The moment is finally at hand.

"You see, being one of the Landvættir is an avatar, a role, a *responsibility*. It is not limited or embodied by a single creature. Should a Landvættur fall, an apotheosis will take place. A new guardian will arise. Gammur has failed Iceland as the current avatar of the North, and now I shall take Their place. While the Eagle lives, the Falcon cannot die. But the reverse is not true."

With that, he whirled and plunged his black blade into the heart of the great Eagle.

CHAPTER

SEVENTEEN

"Noooo!"

Altair screamed as the Eagle's great head sagged on Their chest. The birds above keened and cried out their sorrow. With wings spread in the grip of the shadows Lars had summoned, talons hanging limp, and golden blood dripping down Their chest, Gammur was dead. Everyone present knew that.

"Sacrilege," Magnús choked out, sounding as full of grief as Altair felt. To Lars, he spat, "All of Iceland will curse your name forever. I will see your infamy spread if it's the last thing I do."

The Black Priest did look shaken. He had turned even paler, and his widened eyes darted between the slain Eagle and the man Altair had known as his uncle.

Galdra-Loftur's face was alight with manic glee. He was apparently unaware or uncaring of his follower's shock. "We've done it, my loyal one. What no other has been able to accomplish. The new era of Iceland begins today."

Lars sounded sick as he said, "I-I thought the goal was to trap the Eagle. I didn't know you would k-kill the Landvættur."

"Then you weren't thinking clearly," Galdra-Loftur said. "Disabling one of the land wights would do nothing but buy us a little time. The other three will have felt the Eagle's death and my return."

"They will rip you to shreds and scatter your body to the winds," Magnús said. "Both of you."

Galdra-Loftur just laughed. "I had been told you were dim, but I didn't realize how truly ignorant one of the huldufólk could be." To Lars, he asked scornfully, "How did this one succeed in getting you banished?"

Lars flushed. "It doesn't matter. But he's right, isn't he? The Bull, the Giant, and the Dragon will come."

"Hence all the planning required. I have studied what is known of the Landvættir for centuries. The legends suggest that none of the Four can abandon their posts for fear of leaving the land vulnerable to attack from a cardinal direction."

His grin stretched, lips curving malevolently. "And if it arises that they can come here, so much the better. We have the Shackles and will hold them as easily as we did the Eagle. Moreover, our followers will be ready the moment any of the Landvættir comes north."

The sorcerer turned so that he faced the sea. He gestured imperiously, and the troll holding Altair rose to drag him toward Galdra-Loftur. Altair could hear Magnús struggling anew to free himself, but he didn't seem to be getting anywhere.

Through his tears, Altair glared at Galdra-Loftur. If there was any justice, the hate he was sending to his fake uncle would have withered him where he stood. Unfortunately, it seemed that whatever power he had did not include a killing glare.

"You lied to me for years. Why? Why did you kill my father, and why did you use me this way?"

Galdra-Loftur chuckled. "Have you ever heard the expression that the sins of the father shall be visited upon his child? Fálki stole what was rightfully mine. The things I did to acquire the Rauðskinna, the blood I spilled from my own veins and from a dozen acolytes... I *bought* the Rauðskinna. Then that accursed Falcon got to it first and I could find no trace. In my rage, I made an error. I proceeded with my grand vision—"

"You summoned Surtur. I heard he stomped your ass."

"I called up Satan from the depths of Hell," Galdra-Loftur said reprovingly. "Surtur is just the name the heathens assigned to the Great Beast. But you are partially correct. Without the shackling spell that Gottskálk discovered, the binding was unequal to my vision. Satan came, but He broke free. When He found he couldn't kill me, He turned my mind inside out and threw my body into the sea."

Galdra-Loftur went silent, staring out across the water, his face a countenance of suffering in the rising light of the morning. It was an act for sure, with that bastard trying to look noble or wronged, so Altair remained silent. Maybe the narcissistic a-hole would drop a clue in his ramblings that would help them out of this mess.

"I could not return to Iceland unaided," Galdra-Loftur finally said. "The Landvættir knew me for an enemy and marshaled their minions every time I tried. And so I had no choice but to search through the world for another way in.

"As I wandered, homeless and unwelcome, I founded a new Black School, and I recruited allies. The daubs of magic that touch the world beyond these shores are feeble by comparison to what I can draw upon here. Yet I used what I could. I showed eager recruits hints of the magic that could become theirs, once I conquered. Over the decades, their ranks swelled. I steered them here, but none of the forces, not even Hitler's army, were equal to the task.

"I grew tired of manipulating others to rise against the Landvættir, only to see them fail over and over. Eventually, not only humans came to hear my message." He gestured over his shoulder to where Lars stood, looking uneasy. "Some other exiles from Iceland found me and helped to increase my following. With Lars's aid, I finally reclaimed what had been stolen from me. With that, my path became clear. From a handful of converts, I have been able to grow my own army of humans who want a share of the magic, while my loyal Lars raised support from the inhuman races here."

With that, Galdra-Loftur pointed skyward. He spoke a short spell as he twisted his fingers, and a mass of glowing red energy coalesced around his hand. The energy formed a shape like a bat, then streaked toward the sea. It seemed to bank and follow the coastline to the west, quickly vanishing from sight.

Satisfaction dripped from his voice as he said, "The general of my army is waiting offshore for the order to begin the invasion. An order I have just given."

"Your *human* army?" Lars sounded aghast. "This... They... What have you done?"

Galdra-Loftur looked away from the headland long enough to throw Lars an annoyed glance. "What are you babbling about?"

Lars radiated tension and fury. "You told me we would take Iceland with the rightful inheritors. The huldufólk and others who see the truth, that humans are an infestation."

"And so we shall take Iceland," Galdra-Loftur answered with a grand, sweeping gesture across the landscape. "All of this truly belongs only to those of us who understand the power contained within the island. We shall control its most precious of resources, the magic that seeps into Iceland from the other realms. No more shall we have to settle for weak and thin traces, because *we* shall control the fountainhead."

"I rallied the trolls, the night hags, the gnomes and dwarves. Even some among the dark elves came to my plea. All who were here before Man. I instructed them to capture humans in order to drive the tourists away. Yet you are bringing *more* humans here. You lied to me!"

"I told you we needed an army and so we do. I told you we will rouse the factions here who sympathize with your passion of driving away the tourists and those who don't embrace Iceland completely. And so we shall." Galdra-Loftur gestured dismissively. "Now be silent. I do not wish to chastise my loyal priest in front of others...but I will."

Lars's eyes widened, his cheeks flushed, and though his jaw was tight, he shivered. Lowering his head, he stepped backwards but with a glance first at the corpse of the Eagle.

Quiet settled over the exposed vantage, and Altair could hear only the wind and the keening of the birds still mourning their dead lord. Galdra-Loftur stared intently at the headland around which his signal had flown. Altair found himself drawn, too, anxious to understand what was planned. Again and again, he tried to transform or to speak mentally to Magnús. Something prevented him from accessing his powers.

Perhaps they had died entirely, along with Gammur.

A sob tried to claw out of his chest, but he fought it down. He would not show weakness in front of the monster who had killed the god Altair had been destined to serve, and his father as well.

Grief turned to rage as he imagined Fálki, helpless before Galdra-Loftur. As he remembered his mother's bewilderment and the deep, abiding sadness that had invaded their home when they thought Fálki had abandoned them. And he recalled those years in foster care, the neglect and fear and loneliness.

Hatred such as he had never known completely drowned his grief. If Altair had had a knife at hand and his freedom, he would happily stab Galdra-Loftur.

Just then, movement from grasses a few dozen yards away, near the edge of the exposed area on which Galdra-Loftur held court, drew his eye. Altair focused and nearly gasped in relief as his eyesight sharpened to inhuman levels. His powers were not entirely gone after all.

But what exactly was he seeing? A flash of red fur... One bright, black eye... Pointed, tufted ears sticking up from the head of a, a...

It was a squirrel! A squirrel that was looking right at Altair. There was intelligence and caution in the squirrel's stance. Somehow, Altair was sure it was looking right at him and that it knew him.

The tiny creature moved a bit until Altair could see its red body and full, bushy tail. It twitched upright onto its hind legs, focusing on the sea.

A shout of triumph from Galdra-Loftur drew his attention. The sorcerer was pointing gleefully at the headlands. "There! See, Lars. The captain received my message and is moving into position."

Lars walked forward again, with a troubled glance at Magnús. He stepped right over Altair's legs where he was held down by the unmoving troll. Their eyes met. Lars looked...disquieted.

"Yes, yes," Galdra-Loftur said, all but clapping his hands. "The main force is all gathered here, as I instructed."

Altair focused his eyesight again and couldn't help the groan that came out of him. Dozens and dozens of boats were coming into view, behind a large, white yacht. With the boats were a number of jet skis and smaller watercraft. Each seemed to be jammed with people in gear that looked tactical as well as warm. As Altair watched, the yacht dropped anchor offshore, but the smaller crafts came right up onto the beach. Rubber rafts lowered from the bigger boats whose keels prevented them from making landfall.

Galdra-Loftur chortled like the fool he was. "And these are only the main force. Other factions of the army wait in each of the cardinal directions, in the event the Landvættir abandon their posts and come this way."

"And if they don't?" Lars demanded. "If the other wights hold their position, what then?"

"Then the spell we used to hold the Eagle will serve us again in holding its brethren," Galdra-Loftur answered with a sneer. "Soon we will have the greatest warrior of all under my control, to lead our army. Neither human nor wight will be able to withstand us."

"Oh my god." Altair hadn't meant to speak. He wanted to remain silent, to listen, to look for an advantage. His heart was in his mouth. His eyes lost their odd focus and instead swam with tears. The taste of betrayal burned in the back of his throat, like bitter tea.

Because as he stared out at the flotilla of invaders, at the white yacht, at the jet skis being pulled up on to the strand...he spotted Willa and Jason.

They were part of Galdra-Loftur's army.

EIGHTEEN

Magnús struggled under the weight of the troll's foot that held him prisoner. His ribs felt bruised or broken, and nothing he tried could budge the monster on top of him. His powers all seemed to have fled—he couldn't turn invisible, or reach anyone, even Altair, with his mind.

What had happened to Ólafur, Diwata, and Karl? Had they been captured or killed when Altair was lured away?

He cursed himself for not alerting the others before he followed Altair. In hindsight, it was such a clear trap. Lars had wanted Altair exactly here, where he had an altar prepared for his terrible ritual. Diwata had been right and yet Magnús had not taken the threat seriously enough. He should have summoned help, or called Bryndís at least.

And now he and Altair were prisoners of the worst human sorcerer in Iceland's history, who was being aided by Lars, most hateful of elves. From the argument between Galdra-Loftur and Lars, he had an idea of what was happening even though he couldn't see the water from where he was being held.

He could see Altair, though. He must be as magically constrained as Magnús or he would surely have turned into a falcon and gotten away. Altair radiated distress and misery as he looked out over the Iceland Sea. As he should, upon learning his father was murdered by the man who posed as his uncle. Magnús could only imagine Altair's pain.

Then Magnús heard him say, "Oh my god," and watched Altair's shoulders drop in even deeper despair. He didn't know what Altair had spotted, but he guessed that it was related to the others who must have been working with Galdra-Loftur to steer Altair to this spot.

So many things made sense now. The pressure for Altair to accept a grant he didn't want, the way he'd been led to believe he couldn't return to Boston early... Maybe even his entire university career had been a manipulation. He ached to comfort Altair, though he had no words to make this pain lessen.

The troll keeping Magnús trapped shifted its foot as it craned its head toward the horizon, when dawn had turned the sea to gold.

Dawn... How was this possible? The sun was above the horizon, yet the troll had not turned to stone. He managed to catch a look at the troll holding Altair; the same thing there. How were these creatures able to withstand the sun?

Something nudged his leg then, distracting him from Altair and the mystery of troll animation. He looked down to see a strange little animal. Its tufted ears pointed forward, its tiny paws clutched the hem of his pants. He finally recognized it as a red squirrel. But...what was a squirrel doing in Iceland?

Its black eyes met Magnús's, then it slowly angled its head to look up at the beshitten troll that had imprisoned Magnús. Deliberately, the squirrel moved its head a little from side to side, as if warning him to be quiet.

Magnús blinked to clear his eyes. He knew of no huldufólk who could change shape into a squirrel. What was this creature?

Stealthily, it climbed his leg, moving closer. Magnús remained perfectly still so as not to do anything to alert the troll. The squirrel reached his waist, then it crept up his chest and to his shoulder on sharp little nails. It put its red head close to Magnús's ear, so close that the tufts of fur on its own ear tickled him. And then it spoke, in a whisper so soft it might have been nothing but the breeze.

"I bring news and orders from Queen Hildur. She knows the fate of Gammur. A distraction will occur in ten minutes. At all costs, you are to free yourself and get far enough out of this ensorcelled area to open the Hidden Ways for the queen's army." It clutched Magnús's earlobe with tiny nails and pressed. "The queen directed me to repeat this part of the order. At. All. Costs."

At all costs. That meant leaving Altair behind. Magnús's stomach rebelled. If he obeyed Hildur, could Altair survive without Magnús there?

Diwata's words came back to him, as if the squirrel were whispering again. *If the Falcon dies, Iceland dies. Yet if the Falcon lives, Magnús will meet his doom.*

Was this the moment the Nornir had prophesied? If he obeyed and Altair died as a result, then all of Iceland would fall to the madman Galdra-Loftur or his army. If Magnús saved Altair by his actions, though, then this was when Magnús would meet his fate.

Iceland and Altair. One was the most important thing in Magnús's world to date, and the other was fast becoming even more dear. He did not understand the extent of Galdra-Loftur's plan, but the visions Diwata shared, of death the sorcerer would rain down, had been terrifying. Opening the Hidden Ways, keeping them open long enough for an army to come through... It would drain Magnús. He'd be useless in the coming fight.

But a fight there must be, if Iceland and Altair were to have any chance of surviving. If Magnús had to empty his magic forever to bring an army, or lay down his life to save his country and this human who had claimed a place in his heart, a place he thought no one after Sigurjón would ever touch, then he would do so.

With clarity came resolution. Magnús relaxed his shoulders and nodded slightly. The squirrel crept back down his body and darted away to the grasses, so tiny and quiet the troll never noticed.

Ten minutes crept by slowly as Magnús did his best to prepare. He had no idea what form the distraction would take, or how he would be able to take advantage of it.

Noises had begun to reach his ears from below, where Galdra-Loftur's forces were no doubt coming ashore. Hildur's best chance was to attack before the invaders were ready. If the queen indeed had an army ready, then it was his duty to help her transport it to where the invasion was beginning. Knowing that he would likely have to leave Altair alone with these monsters ate at him. But the situation was too dire to ignore a direct order from his queen.

A breeze kicked up then, but instead of coming from the sea, it blew across the meadow behind him. The breeze became a gale, and then a squall. Rain poured down. In moments, Magnús was soaked.

Lars turned at the unexpected rainfall and said something to Galdra-Loftur. The sorcerer's eyes narrowed. Before he reacted, though, the squall became a tempest, sending Galdra-Loftur's hat out to sea, washing the rocky clearing, drenching everyone.

And the trolls? With a start, Magnús saw that the painted rune of Galdra-Loftur was smearing. The red ink began to run in the rain, and the troll imprisoning Magnús reacted. Giving a bellow of dismay, it rose to its full height, leaving Magnús free. The troll ran, picking up speed as it neared the edge of the cliff. The one holding

Altair saw the first troll coming, and it also dropped its prisoner in order to run.

Too late. The tempest vanished, and the rising sun's rays hit the trolls. Their stride slowed until they were like ants moving in molasses. Between one heartbeat and the next, they became stone.

Magnús scrambled up and ran in the opposite direction. Even though Altair probably couldn't hear it, he sent a feverish message. «Orders from the queen. I will be back for you, I swear.»

Galdra-Loftur roared in fury, Lars was shouting words that seemed like the beginning of a spell, but Magnús made it to a depression between two grass-covered hillocks and kept running.

"Follow him!" he heard Galdra-Loftur order. "Keep that álfar within the barrier even if you have to take his legs!"

Magnús ran faster, aware when the sounds of pursuit began. He was darting along trenches formed between rocky hills, some descending and others climbing, wishing mightily for his invisibility. He dodged around stone outcroppings, sharp edges slashing his face, lungs already aching, heart begging him to return for Altair. The noises behind grew louder. At a guess, three or more pursuers were after him. From the clamor, they must be big.

"Magnús! This way!"

Karl's voice penetrated his thoughts, from somewhere ahead and to the right. Magnús altered his course and made his way toward his friend as fast as he could, with the pursuers sounding like they were gaining on him.

Magnús gasped as he ran through *something* that felt like ice water. In his head, the voice of Ólafur rang out clearly.

«Thank the Allfather. You're out of the enchanted dead zone, and you have your powers back. Keep running, Magnús. Follow the queen's orders. We'll take care of the hafmenn coming after you.»

Struggling to make sense of Ólafur's message, Magnús was

aware of Karl stepping from behind a large lichen-covered boulder, a wooden club in his hand. His shirt was in tatters, blood streaked his face and chest, and his teeth were bared. Magnús had never seen him look so wild. Diwata emerged behind him, pale, blood also on her face and shirt, a dowel in her hand pointed skyward as she chanted. She gestured sharply for Magnús to keep going.

He ran on, though he groaned at the sounds of a fight beginning at his back. If he was to bring through an army, he needed to find a large open space.

Finally, he crashed through a grove of saplings and emerged onto a windswept meadow, dozens of yards across, dotted with hummocks of grass. He fell to his knees to catch his breath and then opened himself to the light of Álfheimur.

As always, the magic was so powerful and purifying that it seared him from the inside. Palms to the ground as he held himself upright on shaking arms, he watched the glow spread until he could see his own bones shining through his skin. The light grew as Magnús formed the glyph with his mind and projected it onto the open field.

The grass, the field, and the ring of thin trees at the edge of his sight moved apart like a curtain. He looked *between* the natural world to gaze once more upon the crystal cliffs and sparkling road of Álfheimur.

Forcing himself to his feet, Magnús stepped through the portal he'd made. For once, it was easy to ignore the singing and the cries of joy from his kin who had returned to Álfheimur. He ran a short distance until his gift told him he had arrived at Queen Hildur's palace at Álfaborg, then opened the other side of the portal.

A host of elves on horseback was waiting. There must have been hundreds of them. At the head of the glorious array, Queen Hildur sat on a sturdy horse equipped for war. Her golden armor gleamed in the light of Álfheimur that spilled through Magnús's portal. Head bare, hair bound into a single braid, Hildur raised her long, thin sword and pointed to the opening Magnús had made.

"Forward!" she ordered and charged past Magnús, through the Hidden Ways and out the other side to the plain of Tröllaskagi. As she passed, the command came right to Magnús's brain. «Hold as long as you can, until every warrior has passed through. We will defend or avenge you and your friends as best we can.»

The host thundered by, three abreast. Light within Magnús burned his bones, and he clenched his teeth to keep the pain at bay. It grew quickly, threatening to take his concentration with agony.

"Hold, my son." Somehow Bryndís was there next to him, cool hands on his burning forehead. Strength flowed from her into Magnús as she worked to ease his burden. Turning her head, Bryndís called out to the unseen inhabitants of Álfheimur.

"Ljósálfar, light elves, kith and kin. The friends and family you left behind on Miðgarður have great need of your aid. Will you set aside your joy for a time and return to the land of darkness and tears? Will you take up the cause of your children and your kind? It is Bryndís Meadbearer who asks this of you."

Magnús fell to his knees, blind with pain. Despite Bryndís's support, he was nearly overwhelmed. Dozens and dozens of elves continued to ride past him in the Hidden Ways. If he failed, if he dropped the portal, what would happen to those in the Ways? He didn't know.

Groaning, he pushed himself to his feet again. He would not fail in this. He was Magnús Bryndísarson of the Hidden Ways, and he would be equal to the task set before him. He spread his trembling arms and screamed.

"Rest, kinsman." The high, lilting voice like a child's came from near his waist. Magnús looked down through eyes narrowed in pain to find a being that seemed to be made of molten glass. It glowed from within, with large eyes that sparkled like jewels. The shape of its ears, the high cheekbones, and proud eyes suggested the face of one of the huldufólk. This beautiful creature resembled an elf no more than one hundred years old, but Magnús sensed it was ancient.

The light elf said, "We come to the call of our daughter Bryndís, and we will sustain the portal. Rest now."

He felt a tugging on the part of his mind that maintained the path through the Hidden Ways and let control slide into the hands of the gathered ljósálfar. The portal between Álfaborg and Tröllaskagi held, the child-elf and others keeping the Ways open with no apparent strain. Running alongside the elven host of Queen Hildur, there now appeared many more of the light elves of Álfheimur. They flowed like a blazing river of crystalline lava, moving with the speed of horses to join the coming battle.

Drained beyond endurance, Magnús collapsed to his knees. His eyes blurred with tears and with pain. Bryndís knelt beside him, again laying her hands on him and sending waves of cooling magic through his heated, damaged bones.

"Well done, my son," she said, and she had never sounded so proud of him. Exhausted, scoured clean of his magic, in a world made of light, Magnús surrendered to darkness.

CHAPTER
NINETEEN

Altair dropped to the rain-soaked ground with a jarring thud as the troll that had been holding him ran toward the sea. Looking around wildly, he saw the other troll heading toward the cliff's edge as well. A shaft of sunlight pierced the rain clouds, striking the monsters. Then the trolls froze where they were, their gray, rocky skin visibly shifting into stone.

Where was Magnús?

A flash of silver-blond hair drew Altair's eyes. He spotted Magnús running, but *away* from them and the sea, past the altar and in the direction of the grass-covered hills that dipped out of sight. Where the hell was Magnús going? Altair swallowed hard. He wasn't *abandoning* the fight, was he?

No, of course not, his heart told him. Magnús was constant, a warrior, brave to a fault. If he was running, it was either to seek aid or get a weapon.

Galdra-Loftur ordered some of those greenish, slimy creatures that Magnús had called hafmenn to go after the elf. Three of them took off, moving faster than Altair would have expected.

"Run, Magnús," he murmured. The sight of the altar, with

the dead Eagle's wings stretched wide, brought despair. Again and again, he tried to change into the Falcon, or to reach Magnús's mind. *Anybody's* mind.

Nothing.

He eyed the distance to the cliff's edge, wondering if he dared to make a run for it, when another of the mermen came to grasp him by the hair. Its slimy fingers ended in claws that scraped Altair's scalp. A smell like rotting seaweed filled Altair's nostrils, making him choke. He grasped at the thing's arm but could do nothing to loosen its grip as it forced him to his knees.

Lars ran toward the two troll statues and went to his knees. With deep sorrow in his voice, he said, "The rain washed away their protective sigil. We should have used something more permanent."

"It scarcely matters," Galdra-Loftur said. "Our army is a thousand strong, even without the hafmenn and the other creatures who are coming to join us. A few trolls wouldn't make a difference."

"It makes a difference to them," Lars said savagely. "And to their families. It will matter to the Mountain King."

"Families," Galdra-Loftur sneered. "Trolls are dumb brutes, good for nothing but their strength. We hardly need to worry about them. Stay focused on the grand plan, Priest Lars. Now—"

From a pocket, the sorcerer withdrew a round stone of some mineral Altair didn't recognize. It was an orb, perhaps six inches in diameter, black but veined in brilliant purple. It looked and felt unnatural in every sense, and Altair involuntarily recoiled.

Galdra-Loftur gestured imperiously at Lars, who rose from his knees and went to the sorcerer. Though he turned his face away from Galdra-Loftur, Lars handed him the Rauðskinna bound in leather made from Altair's father.

Fresh fury and grief washed through him. The betrayal by Trausti, by Willa and Jason...it seemed like bile burned in his very soul. Everything he had thought about them and about his life in Boston had been a lie.

With a golden stylus, Galdra-Loftur etched lines onto the surface of the orb. His marks left behind a shimmer of light, a rune like the one Lars had drawn on the earth before he... before Gammur...

Altair choked back a sob.

Galdra-Loftur studied his engraved orb carefully, comparing it to an image in the Rauðskinna. He nodded with satisfaction, then seemed to study the text more closely. He muttered a few words over and over, as if memorizing them.

Lars leaned in, frowning, apparently to see more clearly what the sorcerer was doing. Galdra-Loftur glared at him and turned away, shielding the orb with his body.

"Beware, Black Priest. This work is far beyond your skill," he said grandly. "For generations of man, I worked to craft this stone. Every bit of knowledge I could find or take, every legend and report of my quarry, the blood of the damned and the innocent alike. I used them all. One being, and one being alone, will be unable to resist this artifact. The sole thing I lacked was the spell of the Bishop's Shackles."

"A spell I delivered to you and tested on yon land wight," Lars muttered.

Galdra-Loftur turned a fierce gaze back upon the elf, who visibly quailed. "Anyone can wield a dagger that has been forged by a master craftsman. That does not make him a master as well. You are just a tool I forged, as is this orb. As is our little Falcon."

With that, he turned to Altair, an awful grin spreading across his face. "You have more innate power than I suspected, Nephew. Several times you nearly managed to free yourself from the enchantments I had that would-be witch place on you in Boston. We had to send other witches to track you and keep the spells in place. Useless, all of them. They couldn't even kill your huldu-maður protector.

"No matter, though. By the time you learned your nature, my plans were unstoppable. My vision is true, and this time I will not be denied."

The sorcerer tucked the Rauðskinna into a pocket of his cloak, then gave a sharp nod to the merman holding Altair. "Bring him."

Galdra-Loftur strode across the field to the edge of the cliff. Altair was again forced to his knees next to him. Below, on the beach, the invading force spread thickly. Altair had never seen an army readying for war, but this was surely what it looked like. Busily, the cultists—or soldiers, or whatever they were—prepared weapons and supplies. Willa and Jason, the bastards, seemed to be important because they were giving orders to other people.

More mermen mixed in with the army, drawing looks of disbelief, wonder, and disgust from the human invaders. All the mermen had a patch or paint on their body, with the same rune in red that Magnús had shown him. More trolls moved on the beach as well, a red blazon on each. Given what had happened to the two troll guards when the paint was washed away, that symbol must be what kept the trolls safe from the sunlight, Altair figured. Perhaps it gave some protection to the mermen as well.

Willa and Jason spread a map on the sand and looked it over with another man. The taste of betrayal sickened Altair. Magnús had been suspicious and had tried to warn him. Was Altair's stubborn refusal to listen because of an enchantment? More likely it was because he so desperately, so pathetically, wanted to believe they were his family.

Galdra-Loftur pointed upward and a bolt of lightning leapt from his fingers to the sky. The flash drew the gaze of those on the beach. When the sorcerer spoke, his volume was somehow augmented to carry words to the ears of the army below.

"My friends and allies. All our decades of planning and all our years of hard work have brought us to this moment. We have accomplished what no one in history has before managed: the magical invasion of Iceland."

A cheer rose from the humans below. Altair noticed the nonhuman creatures remained silent.

"Today, we claim this country for those who deserve to enjoy and exploit the power within the land. Although we have successfully neutralized the Guardian of the North, we must prepare for resistance from the humans who have abused this place for hundreds of years, as well as from huldufólk and perhaps others who do not see that we have the best interests of the country at heart. They have many magical resources at hand, but it will be a day or more before they locate us and are able to reach this spot. By then, we shall be scattered, each carrying out their task to topple the current power structure and install our own.

"Some of you know the great magics that might be arrayed against us, the mobs of elf and wight that might contest, the typical human weapons we might face." Galdra-Loftur paused to laugh. "What good will any of that do, against the greatest weapon on Earth? A weapon I am prepared to bring forth at this moment, to gird you for battle, knowing that with this weapon at our disposal, any resistance will soon wither and fade or die."

Again, a cheer went up. Galdra-Loftur waved to his army, then turned his back to the cliff's edge. He held out his arms, the black and purple stone held on the fingertips of both hands. Closing his eyes, bowing his head, the sorcerer began a whispered chant. The orb glowed softly with a purple light that seemed to come from within the stone, swirling and pulsing in a way that made Altair feel nauseous. Light dripped from the orb to the ground like a fog. This glow was thick and viscous, like it had substance. It quickly formed a pool five or six yards wide. Galdra-Loftur barked a word and lightning struck the pool, turning it black as night. As black as the shadows that had trapped Gammur and that held him still.

Altair's skin tingled from the electric charge in the air. The now-ebon mass continued to swell and thicken. Even though no visible container surrounded it, the substance grew into a column, rising higher and higher. Soon it was at least fifteen feet tall, then thirty.

Galdra-Loftur evaluated the shape, muttered, "More," and spoke another word. The mass spread outward as well as upward until it formed a shape about forty-five feet tall and at least thirty feet in diameter.

Galdra-Loftur carefully placed the glowing orb on the ground just outside the black column. Straightening, he held his hands up to the sky and began a new chant in what sounded like Latin. The hairs on Altair's arm stood on end as chilly sea air grew oppressive and even warm. Lars backed away, eyes wide. The sorcerer's chant continued, each time increasing in volume, until Galdra-Loftur was practically shouting the strange words.

Flickers of flame danced within the column, licking to the edge of the smoke before flattening as if meeting the wall in a container of glass. With a rumbling, grinding noise, a fissure opened in the plain, running right through the area marked by the column. Molten lava oozed up from the crack. The flames within the column increased in intensity, and the ground shook violently. Altair's teeth rattled in his head. He thought he might vomit from the wrongness the sorcerer created.

A boulder at the edge of the cliff rolled loose in the tremor and fell to the beach; sounds of a crash and then screams rose from below. Activity stopped as people milled in alarm or threw themselves flat on the ground, crying "earthquake."

"Stop," Lars shouted. "You'll kill us all!"

Galdra-Loftur ignored him, the cadence and words of his spell changing. The language no longer sounded like Latin, though Altair at first had no guess what it could be. Then his magic, the part that understood the language of elves and birds, translated.

"We met before in contest, and then I was ill-prepared," Galdra-Loftur said. "You bested me and shamed me, destroying my mind. But I recovered, Evil One. Far from these shores, I was carried by my loyal priests and allies. I studied deep magic and lore so that one day I could resume our contest. And the day has come. This is the time when you, the Fallen One, fall still further. Come try me, Father of Lies. Come test your ancient might against the most powerful sorcerer this world has ever produced. Come forth, to be enslaved by Loftur Þorsteinsson, the Black Bishop!"

He stamped his heel four times on the ground. A mass of fire shot skywards within the container. The merman holding Altair was shaken off his feet, Lars cowered on his knees, and cries of dismay came from the beach below.

And then the shaking stopped. The column of fire died away; lava that had oozed from the fissure hardened and turned black.

And standing on the field, atop the ebony-dark disc, was a creature at least thirty feet tall.

Its skin was reddened, its long hair and long beard a brilliant white. It had two arms and two legs, and it was naked but sexless. The face... Altair swallowed hard. The face was that of the most beautiful man he could imagine, but its eyes were far from human. Black horns curled back from its forehead. It opened its mouth, and Altair could see black teeth, sharp and thick. The being let out a roar and raised a fist. It smashed outward but was stopped by an unseen barrier, right at the edge of the black disc that had been a column before. It raised a foot and kicked, but still, it did not get through.

Galdra-Loftur laughed shrilly, hysterically. "I have you, Beast. You are the prisoner and the slave of Galdra-Loftur." The sorcerer spread his hands, the middle finger of each flexed unnaturally, and black shadows swirled up from the disc to wrap around the creature's legs, immobilizing it the same way Gammur had been immobilized. A tendril of shadow continued to climb up the being's massive body. Though it tried to wipe the shadow away, the streak of black entered its mouth. It spat and hacked for a few moments, then froze where it stood, eyes wide and furious.

Galdra-Loftur bent to retrieve the engraved orb. Holding the artifact in one hand, he pointed to one of the troll guards that had turned to stone. "Destroy that," he called to his captive.

Lars cried a protest, but the enormous being gestured. A bolt of fire fell from the sky like a meteorite, striking the stone and shattering it to rubble.

Galdra-Loftur let loose a shout of triumph. He whirled to look down once more upon his army.

"It is as I said," the sorcerer called to the people below. "I, Galdra-Loftur, master of the Rauðskinna, have brought to our cause the most powerful weapon imaginable. I have enslaved the fallen angel, once called Lucifer, and lately known better as Satan!"

TWENTY

Altair stared up at the monstrous captive, bound by black shadows. Satan? It was impossible!

Any more impossible than thousand-year-old elves and ancient sorcerers? his mind yelled back.

Galdra-Loftur muttered something, and a glowing wisp appeared in the air before him. "Join me," he said to it, then gestured. The wisp flew away and disappeared over the edge of the cliff in the direction of the army.

Lars was pacing near the cliff's edge, his face twisted in a grimace. "Human fool," he muttered, his gaze sweeping the beach below. Altair didn't think Galdra-Loftur could hear the elf, but he could, quite clearly. "Mortal invaders. Chasing rumors and fragments of legend. You don't even know what you've trapped. Will the Æsir come to fight Surtur, the king of the fire giants? Is this Ragnarök, then?"

Two people came into view at the edge of the cliff, apparently climbing a path from below. Tears blurred Altair's eyes as he realized who they were. Jason wore what looked like American combat fatigues, while Willa had on a blue cloak.

"As a reward for your service," Galdra-Loftur said, "I will permit you to witness the final phase of my triumph. Perhaps you have final words to address to your charge?" He gestured casually in Altair's direction.

Final words? Altair's heart thumped erratically as his terror built, but rage kept him from giving in. To Willa and Jason, he spat, "You used me."

Jason strode forward confidently. "Hey, little buddy. See? I told you we'd see you soon."

Willa gave Altair an appraising look. "How did you break my enchantments? I put those marks on you a year ago, and they were flawless."

"Yeah, well, I met a better witch," Altair said savagely.

Willa snorted. "Doubtful. Who would want to help you?"

The tone hurt Altair even worse than the realization that Diwata and Magnús had been right about the source of the marks tattooed onto his skin.

"What rhymes with 'witch'?" Jason sneered at Willa and winked at Altair. "At least I don't have to pretend to be her boyfriend anymore."

"Does Professor Milton know what you are?" Altair demanded.

"Who do you think is captaining the yacht?" Willa said. "Milton was a follower of Galdra-Loftur for decades. He brought us into the Black School so we could learn for ourselves the rightness of the Black Bishop's dream. We were chosen for the honor of sheltering you and preparing you for your sacrifice."

"Too true. Of course, we all had to make some sacrifices." Jason rolled his eyes at Willa again, as if trying to get Altair in on his joke.

"You were never a couple. Everything from the moment I arrived at the university was a setup."

"Even before then, really." Galdra-Loftur rested a hand on Jason's shoulder. "Jason was the one who located you in the American foster system so I could come to you as kindly Uncle Trausti. Many years of planning and care to guide you along until the signs were right. And now we have arrived at the most propitious, magical confluence that our dear Professor Milton could calculate."

Galdra-Loftur's grin stretched like a rictus. He pulled his black dagger out once more and gestured to the merman.

"Raise him up."

The merman dragged Altair to his feet, then gripped him by the shoulders and lifted him completely off the ground. Altair dangled there, groaning at the talons digging into his flesh, fear again eating him from the inside. He tried to hold on to his anger, but the blade in Galdra-Loftur's hand terrified him.

What had happened to Magnús and the others? Were they safe?

"Wh-why are you doing this?" he asked, hating how weak he sounded.

Galdra-Loftur came closer and looked Altair over, as if considering the best place to stab. Then he tapped the orb with the point of his dagger.

"This runestone will only contain the Beast for a little while, and I can only control It when I hold the orb. But the bond between Eagle and Falcon... Ah, that is eternal and unbreakable. The Falcon is the servant of the Eagle, and its wings can be clipped unless and until it obeys its master. While the Eagle lives, the Falcon cannot die. But with Gammur dead, you can join him. Then I will become the new Eagle, with Satan as my Falcon to serve me forever."

And he raised the dagger.

Altair closed his eyes, praying to anyone, even the Allfather his friends kept calling upon, that Magnús and the others would be safe. He waited for the sting of the blade, but instead, thunder filled his ears.

He opened his eyes to find Galdra-Loftur, Willa, Jason, and the merman all focusing on the array of rocks thrusting up from the far end of the plain, opposite from the cliff's edge and the sea. The thunder grew quickly until Altair could tell it was not weather but individual beats. A rhythm, a pounding, a crescendo...

And then Galdra-Loftur cried out furiously as dozens and dozens of elves on horseback burst into sight. Among the elves on Icelandic horses, Altair saw glowing, translucent shapes that at first seemed made of liquid, illuminated from within. With his gods-given eyes, though, he could see the figures were of glass, young looking, really more like children. They ran as fast and as steadily as the horses. Were they...singing?

At the head of the cavalry rode a woman, head bare, black hair in a braid, sword raised. Altair had no idea who she was, yet he could tell she was in command.

She gestured with her sword and the elves broke into two ranks that parted to avoid the central plain. Galdra-Loftur looked back and forth between the two phalanxes, as if unsure how to react. Altair thought at first the elves were going to surround them, but then he realized they were heading for the cliff.

They were going after the army on the beach!

Galdra-Loftur cursed and seemed to regain his control. He barked orders to Willa and Jason, who ran toward the cliff's edge. And then he held up the runestone.

It glinted evilly in his grasp as he glared up at the imprisoned monster. Whether it was Satan or Surtur or some other being made no difference. It was powerful and, under the sorcerer's control, it would wreak havoc on the elven army.

Without conscious decision, Altair swung his body back

against the merman that held him suspended, used his feet to push off against the creature, threw his legs up in an arc, and kicked the orb out of Galdra-Loftur's hands.

The sorcerer whirled and backhanded Altair, a ring on his hand cutting a gash. Altair's head snapped back, but the struggle made the merman drop him. He fell heavily to his hands and knees, dazed from the blow.

"Hold him," Galdra-Loftur ordered the merman. He started after the orb until a clamor from the beach drew him back toward the cliff. Altair's head rang—he knew he should try to escape, but he couldn't seem to focus on anything other than the mayhem below.

The elven army on horseback thundered down two steep paths. For their part, the huldufólk were agile and quick on their steeds, some raising crossbows and firing from horseback. Others raised swords or spears and crashed into the nearest humans, trampling and bringing them down. The glass-like figures ran with hands spread; as their fingers touched flesh or fabric, flames erupted. Shouts of dismay and confusion from the invaders went up.

But the invading force recovered quickly from its surprise. Some pulled machine guns and rifles from their landing craft. Others pulled pistols or similar weapons. Then humans began firing on the elves; horses and huldufólk went down. Trolls and mermen joined in, swinging fists and swiping with sharp talons. One of the glassine creatures was hoisted in the air by a troll, then brought down over its knee. The figure shattered into a million shards.

The bareheaded woman who seemed to lead the elven army galloped fiercely through the invaders, cutting a swath that left bleeding and dead humans behind her. She called out a single clear note, and from either side of the beach, other beings joined the battle. Altair didn't know what they were—some looked like the elves but had dark hair and night-black skin. Where they moved, patches of shadow remained. Humans that stumbled into one were trapped as if in tar.

As Altair gaped and watched, he saw other figures, short and stocky, emerging from inside boulders or up from the ground to grapple with the invaders. *Are those dwarves?* Behind the dwarves and dark elves appeared more ghostly figures, tall and willowy.

Suddenly, more humans ran onto the beach but from a different direction than the flotilla had arrived. There were about twenty men and women bearing batons and wearing coats in bright blue and red. Altair recognized those jackets; they were the same ones Karl had been wearing when they met him in Borgarnes. So, these must be members of Icelandic Search and Rescue, and they were joining the fight on the side of the elves.

"Lars," Galdra-Loftur bellowed. "Unleash the rest of your troops."

Almost reluctantly, Lars raised a hand to his temple and seemed to concentrate. Moments later a force of trolls, women dressed in rags, a few elves, and wolf-like beasts came pouring out of various caves. Altair recognized the trolls Magnús had called the Yule Lads.

Another troll, half again as tall and as wide as the others, and with skin that looked black as obsidian, seemed to be leading the nonhuman forces. It had a red bandana around one arm and a skull cap that glimmered like gold in the dawn. Altair saw it look over the battlefield, at the armies of humans and elves, then turn to glare up at the promontory where Galdra-Loftur and the rest stood.

"Lars Berkisson!" the huge troll shouted, loud enough to be heard over the clash of weapons and the rattle of gunfire. "We heeded your words to drive the humans away, not bring more to these shores. What is this treachery?"

"Strike, Mountain King," Galdra-Loftur yelled back. "Slay the huldufólk who have kept you downtrodden for centuries and all will be well."

With reluctance Altair could plainly read on its face, the leader of the trolls—the Mountain King?—turned back to the fight and raised an enormous club. Giving a fierce, echoing yell, it rallied the nonhuman forces and fell upon the defenders like a landslide.

The elven army and its allies fought valiantly, but even Altair could tell that Galdra-Loftur had more people and more deadly weapons at his disposal. Altair wanted to weep. Under a crystal blue sky, beside a glistening fjord, destruction and death was everywhere.

So much beauty. How could these invaders not see past their greed and violence to embrace this country? Why did these defenders have to die to preserve it? He wanted to fight with them. As a human or as a falcon—it didn't matter. The invasion needed to stop! Tears ran down Altair's cheeks, but with the merman holding him captive, he couldn't wipe them away.

"Lars, what are you doing?" The voice of Ólafur made Altair whip his head back from the battlefield.

Ólafur stood alone on the plain, between Lars and the altar. His hands spread wide and a pleading expression filled his eyes.

Lars faltered and his cheeks flushed. In a rough voice, he said, "Have you realized your error, Brother? Have you come to join my —*our* cause?"

"And who is this?" Galdra-Loftur asked silkily. "Another of your brothers, Black Priest? Vörður was a bit of a disappointment in the end."

Lars turned to the sorcerer hastily. "It's fine. Ólafur is sensible and steady. His mind-speech gift is unparalleled. He can be a great aid to us."

"Never," Ólafur said firmly. "You are causing the deaths of the very people you claim are the rightful inhabitants of Iceland. Look at the field, Brother. Elves, gnomes, dwarves, trolls, mermen…they are all dying."

"Alas. I'm afraid your powers of persuasion are not as great as I'd hoped, Priest Lars." Galdra-Loftur shook his head sadly and walked across the grassy field. He stooped, and when he rose up again, the black and purple orb gleamed in his hand. Altair's stomach roiled at the sight of it; he thought he might vomit.

Then he glimpsed movement on top of the altar, near Gammur's corpse. With his enhanced eyes, he focused in and nearly gasped, only choking back the sound at the last second. Diwata was up there, a scrap of black cloth wrapped around her eyes; it had to be the Sæmundur cloth again. She seemed to be searching the ground for something.

Lars was speaking to Ólafur. "Don't be naive. This is war. War for the very soul of Iceland."

"Who are you trying to persuade? I know the depths of your fervor, but this"—Ólafur gestured widely in the direction of the battlefield—"is nothing but murder."

He took a few steps forward as he spoke, drawing the eyes of Galdra-Loftur and Lars. And then Altair suddenly got it. Ólafur was the distraction while Diwata moved stealthily on the altar. He wanted to cheer for Óli, who had bravely walked alone onto a battlefield to face the most wicked sorcerer from history. But at any moment one of them might look up and spot Diwata…

Just then, a figure with red hair, red beard, and a torn shirt ran onto the plain from somewhere below the cliff's edge. He roared and swung the large club in his hand at the merman holding Altair. The swing connected heavily, and the merman groaned as it dropped to its knees. Altair had a moment to realize the new guy was Magnús's friend Karl, now looking wild and animal-like, before Karl charged at Galdra-Loftur.

The sorcerer laughed and made a closing gesture with his fist. Karl's legs seemed to seize up and he fell over, growling furiously.

"A berserkur?" Galdra-Loftur chortled. "I didn't realize any of your breed were left in Iceland, little bear. Well, perhaps you are the last." His mirth turned cruel. "If that's so, then soon there will be no more."

He raised a hand skyward, and sparks danced along the orb resting on his fingertips. An electric charge built in the air, he looked up at the frozen Satan, or Surtur?—whoever!—and opened his mouth to speak.

With a cry, Ólafur flung himself at Galdra-Loftur, wrapping hands around his waist from behind as he pulled the sorcerer off balance. Galdra-Loftur bellowed a curse but quickly worked himself free. He began to kick and punch at Ólafur, who tried feebly to defend himself. Lars stood paralyzed, his face showing his confusion about whether to help his master or his brother.

Through the melee, Altair spotted Diwata pumping a fist in triumph. She was focused at a point on the ground as she pulled an object wrapped in gauze from her pouch. Altair's gaze sharpened even more as he focused on the object. Was that...?

"Hey, boomer Loftur!" Diwata suddenly shouted, at the top of her lungs. Galdra-Loftur paused from punching Ólafur, who lay on his back, his nose streaming blood. Every eye turned to look at the altar and at the witch standing atop it. She ripped the black cloth from her eyes.

"Guess what, asshole? I'm really giving you the finger!"

Laughing maniacally, she threw the mottled, horrible finger of Sæmundur at the ground like it was a grenade.

"No!" Galdra-Loftur shouted. But it was too late. When the bizarre object hit, a silent explosion seemed to go off. White light burst upward and in all directions, illuminating a dome that had been invisible as it sat over the plain like a lid. The dome splintered into a million rainbows, its pieces falling away like stained glass only to vanish before they hit the ground.

A surge of power swept through Altair. He could *hear* with

his mind again. He knew he could transform. Whatever Diwata had done, it had broken the spell that kept him helpless.

Ólafur rolled to his hands and knees and howled in triumph. He sent *something* powerful at Lars's head, a thought so focused and strong Altair could feel its keen edge. Lars crumpled to the ground.

Galdra-Loftur screamed his rage. He swept his hand down viciously; a bolt of lightning shot from the clouds above and hit Diwata where she stood. She went down. Altair had no idea if she was alive or dead. At the same time, Karl launched himself at the sorcerer from behind, biting ferociously on Galdra-Loftur's neck and raking him with hands that seemed enormous and clawed. Again the sorcerer raged, raising one hand to the bloodied wound, making a twisting and hurling motion with the other. Both Ólafur and Karl went flying.

They lay still.

Altair started to transform, but his captor had recovered. The merman gripped his arms, pulling them apart so viciously Altair screamed. He didn't know what would happen if he turned into a falcon. Would the merman rip his wings off?

Galdra-Loftur pointed at the ground, shouted a spell, and stamped his foot. Willa and Jason appeared suddenly, both of them bloodied, with startled expressions on their faces.

"Deal with that witch and these two fools," Galdra-Loftur ordered, gesturing. "I must complete the sacrifice."

Willa and Jason looked around the plain and glanced at each other. Then Willa ran toward the altar where Diwata had fallen, while Jason pulled a large knife from his belt and started for Ólafur's motionless body.

Galdra-Loftur stalked toward Altair where he was held fast by the merman. "Enough delays," he growled. "It is time for the old Falcon to die to make way for the new, the slave of the Eagle forever more." He gripped Altair's hair in one hand to yank his head back and raised his black dagger overhand, ready to plunge it into Altair's body.

A voice came suddenly from close behind Galdra-Loftur, distracting the sorcerer. "The Falcon has his defender still!"

Altair wanted to weep with relief. He knew that voice, would know it anywhere.

Magnús had come for him.

TWENTY-ONE

Magnús stumbled out of the Ways and back to the plain of Tröllaskagi, immediately running to get to Altair.

He was weak from the extended use of his power to open the Hidden Ways. His magic had not had time to replenish, so all he had left was his invisibility, his mind-speech, and the enchanted dagger.

As Magnús broke out of the forest, he saw a flare of white light and a rainfall like shattered glass. Skidding to a halt, he assessed the field. Two humans, a man and a woman, were charging away from Galdra-Loftur; the man went for Karl and Ólafur, who were down, while the woman ran up the altar steps toward a bundle in a cloak. At the same moment he realized that bundle was a fallen Diwata, Galdra-Loftur pulled back Altair's head and raised his dagger.

Drawing on his invisibility, Magnús hurtled toward the sorcerer, hoping the others could help Diwata. His bodily weakness, the inability to call on his magic for any of his usual tricks... None of that mattered. He had to save Altair. He *had* to, and the compulsion had nothing to do with the Nornir prophecy and everything to do with the beautiful, fierce human Magnús had come to know and to love.

Magnús bellowed, "The Falcon has his defender still!" and dropped his invisibility. At the same moment, he sliced viciously at Galdra-Loftur, aiming for the sorcerer's knife hand with Sæmundur's dagger. It glowed brightly, leaving a trail of silver fire as it arced through the air. The blade connected, drawing blood.

The sorcerer snarled when Magnús's strike cut him, but he whirled and threw his black dagger from the wounded hand to the other. He came at Magnús, far faster than expected.

From the way Galdra-Loftur held the dagger, he was apparently proficient with either hand. Plus, he was agile and cunning, quickly driving the weakened elf onto the defensive. Magnús suddenly realized that this human had lived hundreds of years, perhaps longer than Magnús himself. He had clearly learned to fight in an earlier Iceland, a vicious, demanding time and place that had trained him well.

Magnús backed away, drawing the sorcerer farther from Altair. The hafmaður gripped Altair with his arms drawn apart; he could guess that Altair was unable or unwilling to transform to the Falcon. He had to buy time and hope Karl or Ólafur had dealt with the human coming for them and could fight the merman.

The sorcerer feinted. Magnús turned the wrong way and felt the keen edge of Galdra-Loftur's dagger slide across his arm. The burn was worse than being cut; fire and ice seemed to spread up to his shoulder and down toward his hand, making the arm feel useless. The pain made him stumble, and Galdra-Loftur leapt toward him with a cry of triumph.

Decades of battling trolls and other enemies had Magnús instinctively turn invisible and hurl his body in an unexpected direction. Muscle memory saved him because the sorcerer missed and lost his footing in the wet grass that covered the plain.

Magnús, still invisible, headbutted Galdra-Loftur and then swept the human's feet out from under him. Dimly, he was aware of Karl and Ólafur fighting against their attacking human. He heard Diwata shout something—*thank the gods she's alive*—and an icy breeze swept down from the altar at his back.

Focus, he ordered himself and fell on Galdra-Loftur. He knew he couldn't give the sorcerer time to work a spell. He had to fight, for himself, for Altair.

They rolled on the ground, across unforgiving shards of stone and slippery grass, trying for an advantage. Galdra-Loftur had experience, but he lacked the reach of Magnús's long arms or his litheness. Magnús grappled Galdra-Loftur's knife hand desperately as he pressed his own blade downward. The sorcerer's lips were stretched tight in a grimace, his teeth bared. Magnús pressed harder and the tip of the Sæmundur blade inched closer to Galdra-Loftur's throat.

A sudden squall of rain and ice swept the plain, momentarily distracting Magnús. Galdra-Loftur tossed his black blade from the trapped hand to the free one and buried it in Magnús's belly.

The elf gasped, shock immediately beginning to set in as icy fire from the buried blade twisted his guts. He slashed desperately with his own knife, and the blade spread silver fire across Galdra-Loftur's face. Magnús had taken out his eye and scored a vicious wound.

With a scream, the sorcerer got a foot free and pushed Magnús off of him. Pain and ice and agony made the elf collapse on his back, defenseless. But the sorcerer scrabbled away, one hand over his damaged eye. He staggered to his feet, facing away from Magnús, and shouted an incantation. The ice and snow that seemed to be pouring down from the altar formed a whirlwind around Galdra-Loftur. He was lifted right off the ground and disappeared into the storm clouds.

Magnús lay on his back, eyes open to the falling snow. The

pain was quickly fading, becoming something only his body experienced. But Magnús found he was drifting up, above the pain.

From somewhere, he heard Altair cry out his name in fear and rage. The female witch raced by on foot. She was chased by Diwata, who was—oddly—holding a cloth bag.

In the vast, gray storm clouds above, he could almost see someone. A man. A young man with curly hair and shining eyes. The expression on his face was at once beautiful, joyful, welcoming, and yet heartbreakingly sad.

Sigurjón! Magnús cried out.

Magnús, oh my love. This is not your path.

I've missed you, Sigurjón. So much, for so long. I'm sorry I failed you.

You never failed me, but our time has passed, beloved. You have at last opened your heart, and I'm so happy for you.

Sigurjón seemed to take Magnús's hands, but to press him back toward his body rather than draw him up into the sky.

Do you hear me, Magnús? I rejoice that you love again. Your destiny if you remain alive... Well, they've only shown me the smallest part, but it's beautiful. Even more glorious than what I glimpsed when you wove draumagras into my hair. Embrace that! Embrace your Falcon and guard him well. Your future is on Miðgarður, and now your heart is there, too.

Sigurjón released Magnús's hands. They seemed solid, bound to his flesh once more, and the pain was returning.

Don't let go, Sigurjón begged. *Fight to stay there, with him.*

Magnús groaned as the ache in his belly grew terrible. *I...I will try. I will stay here if I can.*

The young man's face was already becoming harder to see. *This is our farewell, Magnús. Know that I loved you truly, and I will take your love with me to my final rest even though we will never meet there.*

Then Sigurjón smiled at him, turned as if to walk away, and

was gone into the storm-tossed sky. Only falling snow remained, and the tears slipping down Magnús's cheeks.

Ólafur spoke in his mind. «...Magnús? Are you all right?»

«Help Altair,» he had time to think back. Then a spasm brought agony to his body and left him overwhelmed.

TWENTY-TWO

"Magnús!" Altair screamed, struggling against the merman that had him. Suddenly, the creature screeched and let go. Altair scrambled away and turned back toward the monster.

Bryndís stood behind the merman, the point of her sword emerging from its breastbone. "Go," she said.

Altair hurled himself away and ran to the body crumpled in the dirt. He knelt, carefully raising Magnús's head to rest on his lap. Quicksilver blood ran from the stab wound Loftur had left in Magnús's belly. Silver-blond hair, dulled with dirt and more blood, covered his face.

"Please don't be dead," Altair sobbed, brushing hair back from Magnús's forehead.

Ice-blue eyes opened slightly. The corners of Magnús's mouth turned in a grimace.

"I did my best," Magnús croaked. "Even though it wasn't enough. You have to save yourself, Altair. Get out of here." He spasmed, pain written across his face.

"I'm not going anywhere," Altair sobbed. "You did everything the gods asked of you. Everything!"

"If you live, Iceland lives. That's what the prophecy said. Galdra-Loftur is wounded but he can't be killed. Surtur will wreak havoc across the land. Maybe the other Landvættir will come, maybe they won't. But while you live, there's hope. So live." Magnús took a shaky breath that turned into a painful, rasping cough. He clutched at his side, above the wound. "Live, for me," he wheezed out, his voice failing. "Altair, I lo..."

The last word faded from his lips as he sank down in Altair's arms.

"No, no, no," Altair sobbed, rocking on his knees as he tried to rouse Magnús. "Don't leave me. You are the guiding star, Magnús. I don't know where to go without you."

"Altair." He whirled his head at the tear-choked alto voice. Bryndís stood behind him, her leather jerkin rent with a ragged cut. Silver blood splashed her cheek and her sleeve.

One hand on Altair's shoulder, she crouched down and rested the other on Magnús's still face. She muttered something in an old language that the Falcon inside Altair barely remembered, something that sounded like a blessing. Or a farewell.

"Stop it, he's not dead." Altair knew he was practically yelling at the ancient elf, but he couldn't help himself. "Save him, please. Bryndís, he's your son. Your son!"

She looked at him, tears brimming in her eyes. "He *is* my son, the best of our race. My magic is great but not enough for this. I cannot hold death back from Magnús even if I hurl myself into Hel first." She took a shaky breath. "But there is a way, I think. One only you can choose."

"What do you mean? What choice?"

Bryndís bowed her head sorrowfully, tears dripping onto Magnús's hair. "I swore to my son that if I could avert the prophecy while saving Iceland, I would. I visited Skuld of the

Nornir and asked how my son's doom could be averted. In repayment of a service I rendered long ago, she gave me the answer. But her answer was a riddle. I only know it depends on your choice."

"Tell me! I'll do whatever I have to do to help Magnús. Don't you know that?"

"Skuld said to me, I see two doors. Behind one, Magnús lies in darkness; behind the other, he soars to glory. Only the child of two worlds can choose which door will open. One offers him a mortal life of freedom and fulfillment of a child's dreams in the land of his mother but will taste of ash. The second will answer his heart's hidden wishes, but his immortal life will be bound to service in the land of his father."

"What...what does that all mean?"

Bryndís met his eyes, her sapphire blue ones reddened with tears. "Listen to your heart, Altair Fálkason. Let it guide you."

"A child's dreams in the land of my mother. That must mean returning to Boston, to my studies. But that life was a lie. My heart's hidden wishes...?"

"Do you know what your heart yearns for?" Bryndís asked.

Altair stroked the head in his lap, running his fingers through Magnús's soft hair. "I do know. But what can the rest mean? An immortal life bound to the—Oh! OH!"

Before Altair knew what he was doing, he had slid out from under Magnús's head, snatched up the Sæmundur dagger, and hurtled toward the altar. Bryndís called to his mind, asking what was happening.

His agile brain connected threads even as he ran. If Galdra-Loftur was correct, the Eagle and the Falcon were more than two physical forms. The Eagle was part of Iceland itself, taking its power from the raw magic of this place and its people. And the Falcon took its life from the Eagle. That was why Galdra-Loftur had to kill Gammur first, because Altair couldn't die while the Eagle lived.

He said to Bryndís, «Before, the Eagle asked me to serve as Their falcon, and to take up Their task if They should fall. That's what They meant! I can take up the mantle of the Eagle. Be the Eagle. And the Eagle must have its eternal Falcon.»

«The Eagle is bound to Iceland, Altair. It is the Guardian of the North. If you become the Eagle, you will never be able to leave this country. You may live hundreds, thousands of years, even. That is what Skuld warns for you.»

Never to see Boston, or America, or travel the world? Never to build power plants, and hope for someone to see worth in him?

Or never to see Magnús again. Never to tell Magnús how brave, how wonderful he was.

How much Altair loved him.

It wasn't even a choice.

As he ran, he could see the battle; it looked like the defenders were losing. A gigantic creature Altair had no name for raked a clawed hand in a wild swipe, and the elf general's horse went down. A force of trolls and mermen clashed with a phalanx of elves and what looked like wood spirits. A female-seeming figure in a robe hurled a ball of fire at a stout dwarf; the dwarf's cloak burst into flame. The human army was running along the beach, armed with guns and arrows and who knew what else. The troll Galdra-Loftur had called the Mountain King swung enormous fists, crushing a being made of glass and fire into glittering dust.

And then Altair ran up the steps of the altar and fell to his knees before poor, tragic Gammur. The dead Eagle's head sagged against Their breast, mighty wings spread wide and held by shadows that writhed and stretched now toward Altair.

Suddenly he smelled ancient snow, heard the creak of ice, and Magnús's voice sounded in his head.

«Don't, Altair. You can't know if this will work. Please, my love. Just run. Escape. Go home.»

Altair darted at the right wing, slashing the shadow there. The silver blade caught fire when it touched the darkness, blazing bright as an arc light. The shadow peeled away, something like a wordless scream rattling Altair's bones, though he could hear no sound from it.

As the right wing sagged, Altair turned grimly toward the second shadow. He didn't know if Magnús could hear him, but he spoke aloud.

"All my life, I was left behind. My father, my mother...they didn't go willingly, but I was alone."

He darted at the second shadow, but it had learned from its fellow monster and it was ready, pulling the wing in its grasp to use as a shield against the knife. Altair stumbled at the parry, and the shadow flicked the enormous wing at him, slicing him with razor-sharp feathers, knocking him to his back. He wiped blood from his forehead and scrambled to his feet.

"Year after year, I searched for a home. For someone to keep me. To protect me and save me. I was so easy to trick, to use. But no more."

As Magnús had shown him, Altair feinted to the left. The shadow reacted, moving again to block his thrust, but tiny, wiry Altair threw himself into a roll, right under the Eagle's wing, slashing at the shadow as he went. The shadow shrank away from itself and from the wing, again with that horrible, soundless shriek as its remnants flew skyward like ashes from a dying flame.

Panting, Altair stood and approached the dead Eagle. With both shadows gone, the body had collapsed and lay draped across the altar. Surrendering to instinct, Altair knelt next to the huge bird, stretched himself across Their breast, and placed both hands on Their heart.

Whatever it was that had made Gammur a land wight still beat there, under feathers and skin and bone. The pulsing presence rose toward Altair's hands, a mass of power that was the thrum of beating wings, the chill of a mountain wind, the roar of an avalanche. It knew Altair and it welcomed him.

"No more," Altair cried again, his voice rising to echo across the altar. "No more running or searching, because I choose *this*. I choose this land and these people. I choose you, Magnús. I am home. And I....am...*THE EAGLE!*"

The words burst out of him with the flare of a new star being born. The power of the Guardian of the North sank into his eyes, his bones, and his heart. It greeted him and sang of wonders they would find and know and protect. Together.

The Land—he felt it to its depth, felt the restless magma and the geysers aching to burst free. He could taste the streams of power from Álfheimur, from Svartálfaheimur, from Ásgarður and the other realms, that brought magic into this singular country. His mind teemed with histories and encounters with creatures of every description, from the smallest lake midge to the mighty dragon Fáfnir. He communed with his new sibling Bergrisi the Giant, fighting Galdra-Loftur's invasion in the South. Dreki the Dragon ran rampant with Their lizards and serpents against the invaders on the shores of the East. The Bull Griðungur charged, leading a herd of creatures in the West.

Altair felt the *wrongness* of Galdra-Loftur's army, the sorcerous threat to everything that was Iceland.

Wings spread wide, he screamed defiance to the sky. His talons raked deep gouges in the altar stone as he launched himself skyward. With a clarity he couldn't articulate, he saw every detail of the battle raging below him, the living warriors and monsters, the dead and the dying.

The Eagle wheeled in the clear, cold air of the North, calling out his summons to his own warriors. Each one heard and heeded the war cry, a million wings taking flight as birds answered their guardian, their master and protector. Great black-backed gulls, arctic terns, ravens, and so many others. They came, they came.

«Altair.»

The word sang in his brain, and he knew Bryndís's voice as the man he had been and the Eagle he now was. That one word was all it took to remind him.

With a twist of his wings, Altair flew toward the ground where a golden woman guarded her silver son, stretched among the rock and grasses. Wind screamed in his ears as he dove, Bryndís and Magnús growing in his sight until he again transformed without conscious thought and landed on human legs.

"Magnús?" Altair called as he went to his knees. He placed a hand on the elf's heart. Words poured out of him like the first rain of autumn, and even if he didn't know their source, he knew what they meant.

"I am Altair the Eagle, Guardian of the North, lord of the sky and the winds, protector of this land. And I tell you I cannot do it alone. You who taught me to love this place and these people—will you join me, Magnús Bryndísarson? Will you bind yourself to the Landvættir and to this mighty work? Will you keep sharp watch and bring me word of joy and threat alike? Will you live while the Eagle lives, soar through the icy air, carry on my task if I should fall? Will you be my Falcon?"

Magnús's blue eyes opened, cleared, and widened. His pain seemed to ease in his awe. His mind opened as well, and Altair could look through Magnús's eyes, hear his thoughts. Could see regal Bryndís, with tears glistening on her cheeks like diamonds. See the glory of the Eagle, wrapped all around one small human. Share the memory of another human, deeply loved and mourned, who faded away into the snow-filled sky, a hand raised in farewell. Hear Magnús's heart leap to pledge himself to a precious, perfect man who was so much more than he knew, even before he sacrificed himself for love of Iceland and for love of a mere huldumaður.

"Yes," Magnús said weakly, his voice breaking. "I-I swear to love and to serve the Eagle as your Falcon. Forever."

Altair reached into his own body somehow, left hand passing through his skin until he held his own essence, his core. It had two pulses, one greater and one lesser. The greater was new, the lesser had been there all his life, though he never knew it until today.

That pulse came loose, and he drew it out of himself. To his human eyes, it shimmered like light seen through the tip of an icicle, fractured and clear and lovely. Through Magnús's eyes, though, it looked like a small sun. It blazed with the glory that was Altair's new country. His land. His home.

Altair lowered the pulse to touch Magnús's chest, then his belly. He released it right over the stab wound Galdra-Loftur had left. The drop of light that was a star sank into Magnús's flesh, drawing the edges of his wound together as it went.

Magnús arched his back and called out, but not in pain. It was joy and life he cried, and then it was the cry of a Falcon in flight. Magnús flashed huge silver wings as he flew upward, a white peregrine with ice-blue eyes behind a sharp, golden beak.

Altair leapt to follow. His wingspan as the Eagle dwarfed his enormous Falcon, but they spiraled around each other higher and higher. Their cries picked up the echoes of arriving birds. Altair turned to wheel and speed over the plain. The thunder of his wings flattened the grasses and stirred sand devils on the beach, knocked human invaders off their feet, and made waves that toppled boats still in the water.

And then the Eagle, the Falcon, and their host of a million birds dove into battle.

TWENTY-THREE

Magnús exulted in the power in his wings as he joined the battle. The weakness he'd felt from opening the Ways, the pain from his arm and from the stab wound Galdra-Loftur had given him—they were all gone. His joyful screech echoed over the sea and against the cliff walls. Many of the combatants paused to look up at him as he passed.

A human with a submachine gun was spraying a troop of huldufólk with bullets. Magnús sank his talons into the man's shoulders and lifted him effortlessly off the field. He winged out over the freezing Iceland Sea and dropped his burden.

Storm clouds still covered the sky, creating wild updrafts. He could *see* them somehow, as well as the lines of magic that tied the storm to a human woman below. He almost went for her before he realized it was Diwata Pétursdóttir. She had summoned another blizzard but was engaged in a magical struggle with a woman Magnús didn't know.

«—That's Willa—»

The Eagle—Altair—spoke the words directly into Magnús's heart. It was entirely unlike the mind-speech his kind used. This was a voice of the wind and the sky, but also of the land itself.

He soared above his lord, the human he loved, the god he served, and watched Altair grasp a good-sized power boat in his talons to fling it against the rocky cliff. At the same time, Altair shared visions to explain everything that Magnús had missed while he heeded Queen Hildur's orders. Altair showed him the summoning of Surtur, the power of the black and purple orb, the way Galdra-Loftur had imprisoned the fire giant with the Bishop's Shackles, the things he'd revealed as he prepared to sacrifice Altair.

In another blink, Magnús explained about being commanded to open the Hidden Ways, the passage of the elven host, the aid of the ljósálfar, and his run back to the plain and the altar.

«I was terrified I would arrive and find you dead at Galdra-Loftur's hand,» he communed to Altair through the flick of a wing, the blink of an eye.

«I feared for you as well, my Falcon, but I never doubted you.»

These words came to Magnús's heart as a particular angle of bank and flexing of talons, before Altair dove to attack the white yacht that seemed to be a command vessel. Magnús joined him, picking one human after the other off the deck and hurling them into the icy waters. The enormous Eagle landed on the very top of the yacht, swinging its huge beak to smash equipment left and right.

Surtur remained motionless on the cliff's edge, flames dancing along his massive body and casting an eerie glow against the bottom of the storm clouds. The birds that had come to the Wind Lord's call were wreaking havoc on the beach. Many had been killed, but more swirled and pecked, taking out an eye here, gouging an exposed face there. Pride swelled inside Magnús. The birds of Iceland were fighting for their land every bit as fiercely as the huldufólk and other allies. Seeming heartened by the support of Altair's avian force, Queen Hildur rallied her troops and the ljósálfar.

«Magnús! The sorcerer returns!» Altair had spotted what Magnús had not: Galdra-Loftur had taken a position on a hill overlooking the beach. With amazingly sharp eyesight, Magnús could see a ragged scar across the sorcerer's face, red and black, but his eye had grown back.

Malice twisted Galdra-Loftur's features as he held out his hands and shouted to the wind. Somehow, he pulled control of the storm right out of Diwata's keeping. The witch stumbled, and Willa took advantage to punch her in the face. Diwata fell to her knees.

Galdra-Loftur twisted his hands unnaturally, and bolts of lightning hurled themselves from the storm to the battle below. Sand exploded near Hildur, knocking her to the beach. Another blast hit the water, where two elves battled a merman; all three were bathed in electricity and sank, blackened and charred, into the waves.

Altair flew at Galdra-Loftur but not before another bolt struck. This time, it hit a troll, one Magnús recognized as Skyrgámur.

The Mountain King bellowed his rage, swinging his huge arms to knock everyone and everything out of his path as he made his way to the fallen Yule Lad. He went to his knees, keening his fury, as he tried to revive Skyrgámur.

«My son, this is a chance,» Bryndís said in his mind. «Quickly, bring me to the Mountain King.»

He wheeled around, effortlessly locating his mother where she stood in leather armor atop the plain. He banked and swept by her, gently grasping her with his talons and lifting her into the air, then releasing her just above the sand at the Mountain King's back.

"Mountain King!" he heard her call out. "You see now the treachery, the evil mischief that has been visited upon you and your people. The human sorcerer Galdra-Loftur lied to Lars Berkisson and thus to all of you. He is not come to sweep Iceland clean of Man but to feed the country to his ravenous followers."

Leaving Bryndís to her course of action, Magnús soared across the beach again, striking at every opportunity.

A clash of red and blue upon the plain drew his eyes. Karl had broken off his battle with the man Magnús now knew to be Jason and charged at Willa where she had Diwata on the ground. Ólafur stood alone, looking terrified at being left to fight Jason, but he didn't drop the sword he had acquired from somewhere.

«I have you,» Magnús sent in the old-fashioned mind-speech as he dove to grab Jason. He was yards away when a bolt of lightning blasted the ground in front of him, nearly singing his wings.

«It's Galdra-Loftur. I'll get him, you help Óli,» the Eagle ordered.

Magnús banked sharply and came again at Jason. He was aware through his connection with Altair that Galdra-Loftur had vanished when Altair was almost on him, only to reappear on another hill. Altair turned in air and screeched his fury, talons out to grab the sorcerer, only for him to repeat his vanishing trick.

Jason kicked Ólafur to the ground, then grasped his sword with both hands, the blade pointing toward Magnús as he came at Jason. But Magnús was too fast. He swerved at the last possible second, dodging the point of the blade but slapping Jason off his feet with a wing. The sword went flying, and a recovered Ólafur brought a stone down on Jason's head. The human was out of the fight.

Magnús wheeled to see what was happening with Diwata, Karl, and Willa. Karl was in full berserk mode, charging and slashing wildly at Willa. She seemed to be protected somehow because Karl's hands, curved into claws, were not reaching her. Diwata was on her knees, apparently trying to work a spell.

Lightning struck Magnús, and he cursed himself for having been distracted from Galdra-Loftur. The pain was fleeting but still stunned him for a moment. He dropped toward the ground until he recovered enough to use his wings.

As he turned to focus on the sorcerer, he watched Altair close the distance...only for Galdra-Loftur to disappear and reappear once again. He was closer to the altar now, in the center of the plain. Altair wheeled and dove again, using his wings to send a mighty gust of wind at the sorcerer. In turn, Galdra-Loftur used his control of the storm to absorb the blast and send it back at Altair. Then he vanished and reappeared almost on top of the altar.

Suddenly Magnús understood the sorcerer's strategy. «No! Altair, it's a trap. Turn away!»

It was too late. Altair was in a furious dive, beak open, wings sending him forward like a meteor. He was ten yards away, five, one, when Galdra-Loftur shouted the words of the Bishop's Shackle spell. The rune that had trapped Gammur was still engraved on the altar, and black shapes raced up the pillars and reached out to grab Altair. They dragged him down to the ground, binding his wings and beak, until he was as helpless as Gammur had been.

Magnús beat his wings as fast as he could. He had to keep Galdra-Loftur distracted and engaged long enough to save Altair from the same fate as Gammur. He flew like an arrow along the plain, pushing his new body to its limits, as Galdra-Loftur raised his black dagger.

A glint of silver in the grass caught Magnús's eye and he thought, *Jason's sword*. Without consciously choosing to do it, he grasped the sword in his talons, flew up to the top of the altar, and cut awkwardly at Galdra-Loftur with the blade.

Galdra-Loftur screamed and ducked. The sword had been able to cut him, though the wound was not deep. Frustrated, Magnús turned back, his great speed making him arc too far before he could reorient himself on the sorcerer. A bolt of lightning struck next to him, then another.

In the air, he was too easy a target and too awkward with the sword. He dove at Galdra-Loftur again but transformed into an elf, the sword in one hand, so that his momentum as he collided with Galdra-Loftur knocked them both right off the altar. They rolled down the stone steps, but Magnús held tight to his weapon.

Both of them got to their feet at the bottom, facing off. The gash Magnús had left on the sorcerer with the Sæmundur dagger had reopened in the fall, and blood streaked down Galdra-Loftur's face.

The sorcerer had just his black dagger against Magnús's sword, but he laughed. "I created that blade. Do you think I will allow it to be used against me again?"

Unnerved, Magnús swung anyway. The sword clashed against the black dagger, sending up a shower of blue sparks. Galdra-Loftur darted at him and nicked Magnús on the shoulder. The pain was less than before but still stung. Teeth gritted, he kept Galdra-Loftur at bay but couldn't get through his defenses either.

At a lucky stroke, Galdra-Loftur earned himself a small space to breathe. He pulled from his pocket the black and purple orb that Altair had shown Magnús. Whirling to face the frozen fire giant, he shouted, "Defend me!"

Surtur turned slowly, reluctantly, but inexorably toward Magnús. It seemed the giant was resisting Galdra-Loftur, which was the only reason the fireball that plunged toward Magnús missed him.

He shifted to Falcon form and darted a short distance, but he didn't dare leave Galdra-Loftur time to increase his control. Altair was trapped still, and the battle between defender and invader raged on. Surtur raised a hand skyward, and another fireball whistled down to smash on the beach, mere feet away from where Magnús flew. The fire killed humans, elves, and trolls, just as Diwata had foretold.

«Magnús!» Bryndís called. «The Mountain King will help. Get him up to the plain.»

Despair wracked Magnús. He couldn't carry a creature as massive as the Mountain King. He'd be burned or maimed. He was useless as the Falcon after all. He was just Magnús of the...

"Oh! That's it!"

He flew like an arrow to the Mountain King, landing in álfur form, and opened his core to the full. The power of Álfheimur roared through his bones. It seemed effortless now, his magic buoyed by the might of the Eagle. Between one second and the next, he opened the Hidden Ways and led the huge troll through, out of Miðgarður and into Álfheimur. The blazing light of his ancestral home burned brightly around him for a moment, and then he opened the Way back to Miðgarður.

He emerged a second later, fifty yards from the altar and just a step away from the disc on which Surtur was still held in place. The Mountain King charged out of the Ways and hurled himself at Surtur, mighty fists swinging into the giant, a creature of earth battling a creature of fire.

"Muspellsheimur shall need a new master!" the troll taunted as he struck.

Surtur defended himself and fought back, but the Mountain King was powerful. They met blow for blow. Galdra-Loftur ran toward the altar, his hand clawing into the gesture Magnús recognized as the one for lightning. He closed the Ways and wrestled with himself on where he should move next. Magnús should have been drained of magic from the stunt, but power thrummed through him still.

On the altar, movement caught his eye. Ólafur turned visible right before the bound Altair and picked up a knife. With stunning clarity, Magnús registered that it was Sæmundur's dagger he held. Ólafur raised it and slashed, then again, then again.

The shadows binding Altair screamed as they died, and Altair burst upward in an enormous blaze of brown and gold. He flew straight at Surtur, calling to Magnús that the Eagle must aid the Mountain King against the biggest threat on the plain.

Galdra-Loftur screamed in rage and made a hurling gesture at the altar. Lightning struck Ólafur, burning his clothes away and sending his body flying backwards.

"Óli!" he shrieked, hearing Diwata keen as well from somewhere near. Shocked, wracked by instant grief, Magnús couldn't move.

Galdra-Loftur turned to face the disc where Surtur was trapped even as the fire giant battled an outsized troll and a god-like Eagle. The disc was covered with shadows, the ones that responded to the Shackles spell. Galdra-Loftur raised his black and purple orb, a twisted grimace on his face, and began to recite the Shackle words. Magnús understood instantly: he was trying to control all three beings at once.

There wasn't even time to move. Not knowing how he did it, Magnús ripped open the Hidden Ways in front of him and behind Galdra-Loftur at the same time. He reached through, grabbed the sorcerer by the shoulders, pulled him into the Ways, and closed the portals.

The crystalline cliffs of Álfheimur, the glimmering light, dimmed. Galdra-Loftur shouted in fury, but the magic of Álfheimur burned away that which was not human. The sorcerer fell to his knees, a black stain spreading from him, corrupting the realm while the realm tried to consume what was left of a human in Galdra-Loftur.

The sorcerer groaned on all fours, writhing in pain, and the black orb rolled away from his smoking form. Magnús lunged for it.

The stone seemed to writhe in his clenched hand, sickly alive and decayed at the same time. With his other hand, he grabbed Galdra-Loftur by the throat and threw himself and the sorcerer out of the Ways, back to the plain of Tröllaskagi.

In the seconds that took, Surtur had knocked the Mountain King to his knees; the troll seemed unable to rise. Altair flew at Surtur's head, raking with his talons, until the fire giant swatted backhand and sent Altair crashing to the ground.

Magnús in human form ran at Surtur, desperate to save Altair. It towered above him, a creature of flame and fury, with power beyond understanding. Yet it was held in place by black shadows that rose from the earth to coil around his legs. And Magnús now possessed the stone Galdra-Loftur had used to command the fire giant to obey him.

"Protect me!" he yelled up at the giant, knowing Galdra-Loftur would come for him as he recovered. A bolt of lightning struck, except Surtur reached out and somehow grabbed it from the sky. The electricity made a ball that sparkled and spat in Surtur's hand a moment, then he threw it directly at Galdra-Loftur. A peal of thunder and a scream of rage signaled the blast had been true but not enough.

What to do? Order Surtur to fight the invading army? Keep him focused on Galdra-Loftur so he had time to make sure Altair was safe?

In Magnús's moment of hesitation, Galdra-Loftur shouted something and Surtur staggered, then fell to his knees. Almost immediately, Surtur rose again, but Galdra-Loftur hurled bolt after bolt at Magnús. He danced between the shafts of death falling from the sky, faster than he'd ever been before, fast as a Falcon in flight. But he knew... One stumble, and he would be finished.

The essence of pine trees, the sound of a brook, brought Bryn-dís's words into his mind. «The orb, my son. Ratatoskur has brought word. You must give it to Surtur and free him.»

«Are you insane?» he thought back, aghast. «The Fire King will lay waste to the entire country if it is freed.»

«Trust me,» Bryndís begged. «Give him the orb!»

A blast struck too close for Magnús to dodge entirely, and he fell to the ground. In another moment, Galdra-Loftur would have him.

"SURTUR! SATAN! Whoever you are!" Magnús bellowed and held the black and purple artifact aloft. The being turned its flaming head, death and fire filling its horrible, beautiful face. "Take it. You are free. Magnús of the Hidden Ways gives you your freedom!"

And with a prayer to Týr One-hand, the god of faith and fools, he hurled the runestone skyward with all his Eagle-given strength.

The stone arced through the air, glittering a sickly lilac. A hand clawed in black steel, burning with flame, caught the orb with its fingertips. It gripped the stone tightly.

"What have you done?" Galdra-Loftur bellowed from behind Magnús. "You can't imagine the destruction you have unleashed."

Surtur raised the steel-clad fist to its mouth and swallowed the stone. All of the flames coruscating up and down its massive body rippled and flared, passing from orange to blue, burning away the shadows that bound it. The unseen column that had trapped it shattered with the roar of a firestorm. The heat pouring off its body increased tenfold.

Battle ceased as both sides halted to watch the king of all fire giants spread its arms wide. Surtur roared in a voice like an erupting volcano.

«—Galdra-Loftur! Twice you have dared the sacrilege of attacking me—»

"It isn't over!" Galdra-Loftur yelled and picked up a stone. "I have the Shackles spell now. I know the rune, the words. You will still be mine to command. You—"

He cut off abruptly and stiffened, his eyes wide. Then he looked down at his chest, disbelief plain on his face. A silver blade, white fire flickering along its edge, protruded from his breastbone.

"Sæmundur's dagger," Magnús whispered.

Galdra-Loftur clutched feebly at his chest and then crumpled to the ground. Behind his fallen body, Lars became visible.

"You brought armies of humans to these shores, false bishop," he hissed. "I trusted you, aided you in every way I could. You pledged to me that we would rid Iceland of humans, and then you brought more and more of them. You murdered my brother and the other creatures of Iceland. Why? Because you thought they were less important than humans?"

Lars leaned forward and spat in Loftur's face.

"This...won't kill me... you idiot," Galdra-Loftur wheezed. "I am immortal."

«—But you can suffer. So come burn forever in my halls, little sorcerer—»

Surtur leaned down, stretching a fiery, black-taloned hand to scoop up the wounded Galdra-Loftur. The sorcerer's clothes burst into flame at the touch. He screamed.

And then Surtur was gone. And with him, the Black Bishop, Galdra-Loftur.

CHAPTER

TWENTY-FOUR

Magnús gaped at his cousin. Lars sneered back. But he walked slowly forward from where Galdra-Loftur had fallen, over the wide patch of burnt grass, to present Sæmundur's dagger, hilt first, with a slight incline of his head.

Fresh rage surged through Magnús as he took the weapon. Ólafur was dead and it was Lars's fault. Here was the perfect opportunity to, finally, avenge himself upon the murderer of Sigurjón, the killer of Óli and Gammur, the betrayer of Iceland. Lars wasn't even trying to defend himself. He just stood there, arms limp in his black robe, and stared Magnús in the eye.

Magnús recalled his long-ago promise to Queen Hildur, not to kill except in immediate peril. How easy it would be to say that Lars had attacked him, to justify the killing blow... Lars almost seemed to be daring him to do it.

Though his hand clenched tightly on the hilt of Sæmundur's dagger, Magnús hissed, "I will not end your shame so quickly. The queen's justice will determine your fate, blasphemer."

Turning away, blade in hand, Magnús ran up the steps of the

185

altar and quickly used the dagger to scratch out the rune of the Bishop's Shackles before tucking away the enchanted weapon. Altair landed behind him in human form.

Magnús turned and took Altair in his arms. They held each other tightly, the tall elf and the slender human.

"I'm so sorry about Ólafur," Altair whispered, his voice thick with tears.

"Not yet. Please," Magnús begged. "I can't think about him until this is finished."

Altair rubbed his head against Magnús's chest. "I know. I was so afraid for you," Altair mumbled. "But I could *feel* you fighting, and your bravery."

"If I was brave, it's because of you." Magnús put his finger under Altair's chin to raise up his head. He leaned down and pressed their lips together. Altair moaned against his mouth and tightened his grip.

The kiss was everything Magnús had imagined, full of warmth and passion. He could taste Altair's fierce pride, could smell the ocean wind in his hair, could feel the power and love that thrummed beneath his skin.

He leaned back, meeting Altair's eyes, which were completely golden now. The enormity of what had happened—what they had both become, what they had lost—washed over Magnús and sent a shiver down his spine. Their minds and hearts were linked so there was no need to say anything to Altair; the new Eagle simply nodded his head in agreement.

"I know. Me, too."

"Can you feel the Rauðskinna?"

Altair cocked his head and looked around. He shook his head. "I don't sense anything. Galdra-Loftur had the book in his pocket, so it's probably in Hell or Muspellsheimur with him. I'm still confused about that."

Movement drew their eyes at the same time. Ólafur, his naked skin reddened with awful burns, pressed a hand to his eyes and groaned. A silver chain with a pendant stone hung around his neck, though his clothing was mostly destroyed.

"You're alive!" Magnús cried, throwing himself to the ground by his cousin. He wanted to touch, to help, but the burns looked so painful...

Altair fell to his knees beside Ólafur and closed his eyes. Radiance grew from his hands until white light shone from beneath his skin. A gust of wind swept past the Eagle, bringing the smell of clean winds and snow. Just like Gammur's presence had healed him after the first skirmish on the beach, Magnús felt his pains ease. He watched in wonder as the angry red burns on Ólafur's body faded to pink, then became pale skin.

Altair dropped his hands and opened one eye. "Did it work?"

Magnús grabbed Altair tightly. "Thank you, my love. You are..."

Words failed him and so he opened himself to Altair as fully as he could. The only gift he had worth sharing was his heart and his truth, and he gave them freely, huldumaður to human, Falcon to Eagle, man to man. All his loneliness and doubts, his anger and his passion for Iceland and its people, the special place Sigurjón had in his memories, the new love that had taken root for Altair.

"You've been alone," Altair whispered, sounding so sad Magnús had to kiss him again. Though speechless, Altair could still reach Magnús's mind as they kissed. «You aren't alone anymore. You don't have to save Iceland by yourself, Magnús. You have so many people in your corner—Bryndís, Ólafur, Diwata, Karl...and me.»

Footsteps running up the altar steps made them both turn. Diwata went to her knees beside Ólafur, weeping. "You're alive. Oh, thank the gods."

"Your charm," Ólafur said hoarsely, gesturing feebly at the

pendant around his neck. Diwata nodded slightly, eyes squeezed shut as she held on tightly to Ólafur.

Karl appeared right behind her, his voice grim as he said, "I'm happy you're all alive, but we need you. The battle isn't over."

Altair and Magnús looked at each other and at their friends. They had all taken many hurts, risked their lives, paid greatly to save their beloved country. And it was time to finish together, in the light, what they had begun together in midnight darkness.

Eagle and Falcon nodded with shared determination and melted skyward in their new magical bodies. In perfect harmony, they assessed the battlefield. Jason lay clawed and bloody, his eyes open to the sky. Willa was bound and on her knees, seeming helpless with a bag over her head. But the invading army didn't yet know that Galdra-Loftur was gone and so it fought on.

With a cry to rally the birds and to inspire the defending huldufólk, ljósálfar, and other denizens of Iceland, Altair swooped to attack the ground troops. Magnús harried the boats that remained offshore. Together, they quickly sank the yacht.

The Mountain King recovered his feet. He staggered to the edge of the plain overlooking the beach and bellowed to the nonhuman forces that survived to stop fighting. After that, the invaders quickly surrendered. Humans dropped weapons or simply sank to their knees on the wet and bloody black sand. Corpses floated in the sea or lay on the beach.

The sounds of grief were everywhere as comrades discovered the fate of friends and family. And cries of agony also rose, from the wounded. Altair's feathers ruffled and a white glow spread from his wings. He flew slowly over the battlefield, around and around, back and forth over the wounded until their moans faded, first to whimpers and then to relieved calm.

But a swell of relief and joy grew in place of pain. Queen Hildur raised her sword wearily in salute to the Eagle and the Falcon where they wheeled in the sky. Shouts of thanks rose from her troops. It would have brought tears to Magnús's eyes if he'd been in álfur form.

He landed on the beach before Hildur, next to Altair. Only then did he realize that they remained clothed in these shapes. He caught Altair's eye, who thought to him, «We're getting better at this all the time.»

Queen Hildur dismounted and handed the reins of her horse to Bryndís. Magnús started to bow, but Hildur went down to one knee before them both. Bryndís, too, lowered herself to the ground, and then a ripple spread as all the remaining defenders, with the nonhuman invaders who had surrendered, followed suit. The ljósálfar kept to their feet but burst into a song of joy and light.

Altair blinked in astonishment, looking across the sea of people paying homage.

«You are Landvættur now, Altair,» Magnús told him. «One of the most beloved figures in our world and a hero in your own right.»

Altair looked up at him, those golden eyes blurring with tears. «You are the hero, Magnús. You and Ólafur. You kicked Galdra-Loftur's ass and freed Surtur. Óli saved me nearly at the cost of his life. You even gave up the chance to be with Sigurjón.»

«Sigurjón was my past, and I will always honor his memory. You are my love, Altair, now and for as long as we remain. And you sacrificed everything you held dear to save Iceland and to save me.»

Altair gave a small, shy grin. «I guess we'll have to continue this debate of who is the bigger hero later. I think the queen wants to address us.»

Hildur had indeed regained her feet. "Wind-wingéd Eagle. Hope-bringing Falcon. We praise and honor the Landvættir who have once again saved all of Iceland from invasion. The wounded and the fallen must be dealt with, with your leave, and then we would hear the judgment of the Eagle upon the invaders who live."

Bryndís spoke softly. "My lords, Ratatoskur brought word of other invasions and battles with thy brethren Landvættir. Is it your wish that we aid them?"

Magnús asked, "Ratatoskur?"

At the same time, Altair closed his eyes and shook his head. "All is well. The Bull, the Dragon, and the Giant faced smaller forces, and they have triumphed." He smiled slightly, tilting his head down. "They send greetings to their new brother and to his chosen champion, and their thanks to the ljósálfar who aided Iceland in its hour of need."

The child-elf Magnús had seen in the Hidden Ways came forward, and a gentle laugh fell from her lips. "Paradise is all the sweeter for a brush with danger and with the children we left behind. Those huldufólk who fell today will never join us, but they will be remembered forever in song and story. We grieve with you, but do not let your grief dim the light in your heart."

She gestured, and a portal opened. Glorious light and song spilled onto the blood-drenched beach and bounced off the storm clouds above. Ljósálfar ran through the opening swiftly, calling their farewells and good wishes.

The last to leave was the child-elf, who paused to rest a hand on Magnús's arm. "Thou art a descendant of the body I left behind in Miðgarður long ago. Come visit us, great Falcon. Thou wilt find the Hidden Ways far easier to bear, now that thee are companion to a god." She stepped through and the portal closed, dimming the beach.

Bryndís gestured at someone behind Altair and Magnús. "My dear, will you release your storm and let us see what more healing is required?"

They turned to find Diwata standing near, flanked by Karl

and a clothed Ólafur. At Diwata's feet was Willa, her head still encased in a sack. Magnús raised his eyebrow in question.

Diwata said grimly, "I remembered this from when we studied the Sagas in school. Throwing a sealskin bag over the head of a witch was known as a way to prevent them from using magic."

She looked up at the clouds, raised her quartz, and muttered a spell of release. Magnús realized he could understand the words now. The storm clouds dissipated quickly, bringing the light of the risen sun to spill down upon the battlefield.

Magnús looked around in dismay, and he could feel Altair's grief as well. The wounded were greatly healed by the Landvættur's power, but Altair could not raise the dead. Thousands of birds had given their lives to defend Iceland, and there seemed to be hundreds of bodies—humans, huldufólk, hafmenn, dvergar, and others.

As many as three hundred human invaders stood huddled together in groups, guarded by the defenders. Rage over the carnage the invasion had wrought swept through Magnús. He wanted to speak, but Altair put a hand in his. At the touch of his Eagle, calm melted Magnús's anger and he remained silent.

Altair's voice rang out across the beach. Magnús heard the words in many languages at once; gods, there was much to learn about their new powers, though Altair seemed to manifest them naturally. Pride in Altair swelled Magnús's chest as the Lord Eagle dispensed justice.

"You invaders came looking for power, following a madman who would have delivered this country to evil and slavery. You will remain here long enough to bury the dead, both those who deserve the highest honors and those of your army whose names will be forgotten. And then you will leave these shores forever, to remind those who would challenge Iceland that it is protected by forces unknowable and to stay away."

Queen Hildur bowed her head in agreement. "The Eagle is just and merciful. It shall be done."

She indicated three of her retinue, who immediately organized groups to oversee the losing army as it buried the dead.

Bryndís spoke again. "You asked about Ratatoskur, my son... Pardon, my lord."

"Please, Mother. I remain your son," Magnús said.

"Very well. May I present the Lord Ratatoskur."

The red squirrel bounded up Bryndís's arm to her shoulder and rose up on hind legs. It peered intently at them.

Altair inclined his head gravely. "Welcome, Ratatoskur, and our thanks for the aid you rendered. I did not recognize you before I became the Eagle, but now I know you well."

Turning to Magnús and his friends, Altair smiled. "Do you recall the words from the Prose Edda that you all shared with me when I first became the Falcon?"

Ólafur grinned and recited, "'A squirrel, by name Ratatoskur, springs up and down the tree, and carries words of envy between the eagle and Níðhöggur.'"

The squirrel spoke in a piping trill. "Not merely words of envy, though I do love to rile up the old Serpent. It resides between worlds, here manifesting in Álfaborg. I carried word of the blasphemy upon the Eagle and of the invasion back to Níðhöggur and to Hildur and brought their instructions to you."

"He told us what to do as well," Karl said. He bowed to the squirrel, then grinned at Magnús. "Bjarni will not believe the story I have to share with him."

Magnús reached out and pulled Karl into a hug. "I am glad you're safe, my friend. I didn't get the opportunity to tell you properly before." He turned and gestured to Altair, who stepped closer, hand outstretched. "Altair, do you remember my friend Karl who took up the search for the trolls?"

Karl took Altair's hand gingerly in both of his and bowed his head.

"I'm glad to meet you again," Altair said, smiling. "There's so much knowledge filling my head that I haven't been able to sort it all out yet, but what is a berserkur?"

"Apparently that's me." Karl shook his head. "I had no idea. And frankly, I don't know what it means." He looked down at his hands, again normal but covered in blood. More blood stained his torn shirt.

"It means you're a badass," Diwata said. To Altair and Magnús, she explained, "When you both disappeared from the beach earlier, it was Karl who figured out what to do. He called in his SAR colleagues from Akureyri, too. We gathered pretty quickly that there was a spell over that area with the altar that prevented magic unless you had that symbol from Galdra-Loftur on your person. Karl and Ratatoskur came up with the plan for me to make rain and create the distraction that let you get away, elf boy."

She looped one arm through Karl's and the other through Ólafur's, who blushed as he stepped closer to the witch. "Óli, though, had the idea of using Sæmundur's cloth and finger. He knew Lars was good with illusions, so he figured the rune Galdra-Loftur used for his spell would be hidden that way. With the cloth, I could see through Lars's illusion and then break up the rune with Sæmundur's relic."

"Regarding Lars Berkisson..." the queen said and gestured. Two of the huldufólk led Lars forward. His arms were bound, and a look of defiance mixed with fear distorted his once-handsome face.

Magnús quivered with remembered rage. Again, Altair's cool voice entered his head, soothing him. «He must be punished, but not by us. Let the queen decide.»

Magnús took a deep, shuddering breath. If the queen had

listened to him after Sigurjón and put Lars to death, would all of this have been avoided?

«Only the Nornir know. He turned on Galdra-Loftur and gave us the victory. That small drop must be weighed in assessing the evil he caused.»

Magnús nodded slowly, then shared a glance with Altair. «You've become wise so quickly, little bird. Are you sure you're an Eagle and not an owl?»

Altair laughed out loud, and Diwata grinned. "Gonna share the joke with those of us who don't speak Bird?"

"Nope," Altair said cheekily, and that made Magnús's heart leap. The eager, funny human he'd fallen in love with was still there in Altair, despite the godhead that had fallen upon him.

Turning to Hildur, Altair said, "The Landvættir leave the fate of Lars Berkisson and his cohorts in the judgment of the queen of the huldufólk."

She nodded regally, Queen to the Elves addressing the Lord of the Northern protectors, then beckoned for Lars to be brought forward. "Will you speak in your defense?"

Lars shook his head defiantly.

"Your Grace, with permission?" Ólafur said. Hildur gestured for Ólafur to go on. "My gift, as you know, is to see into the mind. Lars is my kin, but that does not cloud my words.

"He is full of shame for the deaths he has brought to the inhabitants of Iceland, to the huldufólk and the trolls and the hafmenn and so many others. He knows the blasphemy he committed against the Landvættir. Where once he was righteous in his condemnation of humans, he has come to see the valor of those who defend our country." Ólafur paused. "And he is furious with me for revealing all this."

To Lars, who was glaring at him, Ólafur said, "You are my brother. Since you will not speak up for yourself, I must speak for you."

Lars dropped his head, moving his shoulder as if to wipe away tears. He murmured, "I...rejoice that you were not killed. Brother."

Magnús didn't know what to think. He had hated Lars for so long. Had wanted his vengeance, *demanded* it even. Nothing would erase the harm Lars had caused, but it was Magnús's righteous anger that led to Lars being cast out into the human world where he encountered Galdra-Loftur. Magnús must accept his own role in the path of Lars's life.

"Your Grace," he said, before he'd been aware he would speak. Hildur looked at him curiously. "You are well aware of the history between Lars and myself, and perhaps you expect me to seek his death once more. But I do not ask for that. Lars has covered himself in shame and in the blood of his people, indeed, the people of all Iceland. As my Lord Eagle has said, we leave his judgment in your hands. But my *request* is that you consider your own history and whether that suggests an appropriate punishment."

Hildur nodded thoughtfully. "Yes, I see what you mean. Very well. Lars Berkisson, this is our judgment.

"Your prejudice against humans has brought death and destruction to every element of our world. Rather than take your life, then, I will ensorcel you as I was once ensorcelled. You shall be made human, your gifts and your grace removed from you, and you will be unable to reveal that you were ever of the huldufólk. One night a year, on the Yule, your nature will return for the span of eight hours, to remind you of what you have forfeited by your actions. Your memories and shame I leave you, and also the possibility of a good human life. Perhaps you will fall in love with a mortal and have mortal children as I did long ago. If, before you die a mortal death, you can persuade one member of each of the races of Iceland to forgive you, your punishment shall be lifted."

Lars cleared his throat. "I accept the judgment of Queen Hildur, and the mercy of the Landvættir." He shot a fleeting glance at Magnús, then looked down again and whispered, "I will endeavor to make amends in the lifespan I am allotted."

Bryndís rested a hand on her nephew's shoulder and led him away.

The queen said, "And now for those who allied with Lars and Galdra-Loftur."

The Mountain King forced his way through the soldiers and survivors until he was staring down at Hildur. His golden skullcap was dented and tarnished with blood, his obsidian skin was chipped and shattered in places, but he glared fiercely, King to Queen.

"The trolls deny your right to pass judgment. Huldufólk had as much to do with these events as any of the races of Iceland."

Hildur flushed and opened her mouth to argue, but a proud-looking dvergur Magnús did not know emerged from the crowd. She wore no insignia of office, but her manner indicated she was a leader. "We agree with the Mountain King to this extent. There is blame and praise to be shared. The dwarves call for an Alþingi of Realms to consider these matters."

One of the dark elves who had fought with Hildur's forces also spoke in agreement, and members of other races murmured as well.

Hildur sighed but capitulated with seeming grace. "Very well."

She returned to looking over the human invaders and paused when she came to the bound Willa.

"My Lord Eagle," Hildur said, "Lord Ratatoskur has told me of your specific betrayal by three among the invaders. The ones named Milton and Jason are dead. Only this witch remains. What is your will in her fate?"

Altair opened his mouth to speak, but Diwata jumped in. "Your Grace, as she is a human witch and has worked evil magic in our country, I request that you leave her fate in the hands of the seiðmannaþing."

"I agree," Altair muttered, seeming relieved. To Magnús, he thought, «I know what Willa did. That none of it was real to her. But...it was real to me. She and Jason gave me a home of sorts. Professor Milton gave me a purpose. They had agendas and they lied, but those years meant everything to me.»

«I understand,» Magnús answered. «Your own home was stolen from you, but in their small way, they let you find a new one. A family that you have given up for me and for Iceland.»

Altair looked up at him quickly, golden eyes glowing.

«I gave up nothing, but I have found everything,» he thought fiercely. «I love you, Magnús. And I love this magical country. I struggled for years to fit in, to be what they wanted me to be so that I could stay. And then I came here, where I am loved for who I am. Family? That's the people you will do anything for, and who will do anything for you. *You* are my family, with Diwata and Ólafur and the others. This is my home now, and I will protect it to my last breath.»

At that, Altair erupted upward in an explosion of wing and talon, crying out love for his adopted land as he wheeled skyward.

Magnús followed, sharp eyes scanning the country below even as wind currents and joy bore them to the North, the Eagle and the Falcon, mighty guardians of fabled Iceland.

GLOSSARY

Terms, locations and gods appearing throughout FALCONSAGA:

Æsir: the principal pantheon of Norse gods

Akureyri: the second-largest city in Iceland, located to the north of the island

Álfaborg: the capital city of the huldufólk where Queen Hildur maintains her court; located beneath a hill in the human town of Borgarfjörður-Eystri

Álfar: (singular, álfur) the light elves from Álfheimur, also known in Iceland as the huldufólk

Álfheimur: one of the Nine Realms, the original home of the álfar or elves

Alþingi of Realms: a gathering of leaders from each of the Nine Realms to establish laws and adjudicate matters that affect more than one race of beings in Iceland, inspired by the first human parliament, called Alþingi

Ásgarður: one of the Nine Realms, the home of the Æsir

Askur and Embla: the first humans on Miðgarður, fashioned from an ash and an elm tree by the gods Óðinn, Vili and Vé

Bergrisi: one of the four Landvættir or land wights, in form a giant that guards the south of Iceland against sorcerous invasion

Berserkur: term used for Norse fighters renowned for their bear-like strength and ferocity, derived from certain humans who could channel the power of a bear more literally

Black School, The: in legend, a school created by the Devil to train magicians

Borgarnes: a town north of Reykjavik, in a region where Egill Skallagrímsson, the poet-hero of Egil's Saga, had a farm

Brennivín: a clear, herbal, distilled liquor made in Iceland, usually from caraway or dill

Dimmuborgir: an unusually shaped lava field near Mývatn in the eastern part of Iceland, composed of volcanic caves and rock formations

Dökkálfar: (singular, dökkálfur) the dark elves from Svartálfaheimur, who have power over shadows and are close kin to the álfar

Draugur: an undead creature, something between a ghost and a ghoul

Draumagras: Icelandic name for a magic plant called dream grass; when woven into the hair before sleep, it brings answers to questions or dreams of the future

Dreki: one of the four Landvættir or land wights, in form a dragon that guards the east of Iceland against sorcerous invasion

Dvergar: (singular, dvergur) the dwarves from Niðavellir, who can move through solid stone

Egil's Saga: one of the great Icelandic family sagas, about the life of Egill Skallagrímsson

Egilsstaðir: a large town in the east of Iceland

Eir: the goddess of healing

Eyrbyggja Saga: one of the Icelandic sagas, about a long-standing feud between two chieftains

Fáfnir: one of the dvergar who became a dragon and now guards his golden hoard somewhere in Iceland

Fenrir: a monstrous wolf and son of Loki, who is foretold to kill Óðinn during Ragnarök

First Covenant: a law made at the original Alþingi of Realms, which states, "No being not of Iceland shall be told of or allowed to spread knowledge of Iceland's super-nature."

Forseti: the god of justice and reconciliation

Freyja: the goddess of magic, love, and fertility; one of the Vanir rather than the Æsir

Freyr: the god of fertility, good harvest, and prosperity; one of the Vanir rather than the Æsir

Galdra-Loftur Þorsteinsson: a human sorcerer who lived in the seventeenth century and practiced evil magic; reputedly immortal, last seen when cast in the sea by the Devil after failing to enslave him

Galdrabók: Icelandic for a spell book or grimoire

Galdur: a form of Icelandic magic using incantations

Gammur: one of the four Landvættir or land wights, in form a giant eagle that guards the north of Iceland against sorcerous invasion

Goði: a male chieftain; ; *see also* Gyðja

Gráskinna: a galdrabók reputed to contain many evil spells but not as dark as those in the Rauðskinna; also called the Gray Book

Griðungur: one of the four Landvættir or land wights, in form a giant bull that guards the west of Iceland against sorcerous invasion

Grýla the Trollmother: a troll reputed to make a soup from the bodies of naughty children, who are found and brought to her by the Yule Cat

Gyðja: a female chieftain; *see also* Goði

Hafmenn: (singular, hafmaður) a sea-creature that can live and fight in the water or on land, an Icelandic merman

Hafnarfjörður: a town south of Reykjavik, known for its population of elves

Hákarl: fermented shark, a national dish of Iceland

Hallgrímskirkja: a Lutheran church in Reykjavik, the largest church in Iceland and one of its tallest buildings

Hamarinn: a city of the huldufólk, located beneath a park of the same name in the human town of Hafnarfjörður

Harpa: a concert hall in Reykjavik

Heimdallur: the god of foreknowledge who protects the realm of Ásgarður

Hel: the goddess of death and a daughter of Loki, who rules an area—also called Hel—that is located in the realm of Niflheimur

Hermóður: the god of messengers

Hidden Ways: magical paths that connect Miðgarður to Álfheimur, and perhaps to other of the Nine Realms

Hólar: a town in the north of Iceland

Huldufólk: (singular, huldumaður, huldukona) Icelandic for "hidden folk", the term that álfar in Iceland use for themselves, signifying their ability to turn invisible at will

Jólaköttur: the Yule Cat, a giant black cat that searches for children who have not been given a gift of clothing for Christmas (and hence are unruly or lazy) and brings them to Grýla Troll-mother to cook into her stew

Jötunheimar: one of the Nine Realms, and home to the jötnar or frost giants

Keflavik: the international airport located near Reykjavik

Kjaftæði: Icelandic for "bullshit"

Landvættir: (singular, Landvættur) Icelandic for "land wights", the four mystical protectors of Iceland

Ljósálfar: (singular, ljósálfur) the light elves who reside in Álfheimur rather than on Miðgarður

Loki: the god of mischief and sorcery

Manngjöld: a payment made in compensation for taking a life

Meili: the god of travel

Miðgarður: one of the Nine Realms, also known as Earth; home of humans, trolls, and certain wights or spirits

Mímir: the god of wisdom

Moðormur: a worm-dog with an all-black or all-white body but red paws; its gaze is deadly

Mountain King: title of the ruler of the trolls of Miðgarður

Muspellsheimur: one of the Nine Realms, home of the eldjötnar or fire giants; ruled by Surtur

Niðavellir: one of the Nine Realms, home of the dvergar or dwarves

Níðhöggur: a serpent that lives at the base of Yggdrasill and exists in multiple realms at once

Niflheimur: one of the Nine Realms, where some of the dead go; ruled by Hel

Nine Realms, The: the nine worlds connected by Yggdrasill

Nornir: three sister goddesses of destiny, who weave fate near the Well of Urður at one of the roots of Yggdrasill

Nykur: a water spirit, sometimes appearing as a horse

Óðinn: chief of the Norse pantheon, leader of the Æsir; also referred to as the Allfather

Pabbi: Icelandic term of endearment for a father

Plokkfiskur: an Icelandic dish of potatoes mashed with cod

Ragnarök: also called the Twilight of the Gods, the last battle between the Æsir and the forces of evil

Ratatoskur: a squirrel that runs up and down the branches of Yggdrasill, bringing news and messages to, among others, Gammur and Níðhöggur

Rauðskinna: a galdrabók reputed to contain many evil spells; also called the Red Book

Reykjanes: a peninsula south of Reykjavik with frequent volcanic activity

Reykjavik: the capital city of Iceland

Ring Road: a highway that circles the perimeter of Iceland

Sæmundur: an Icelandic bishop and hero of many folktales, sometimes referred to as the wisest human in Icelandic history

Seiðmannaþing: the council of witches

Seiður: a form of Icelandic magic using rituals

Skagafjörður: a fjord in the north of Iceland, not far from Hólar

Skalla-Grímur Kveldúlfsson: the father of Egill Skallagríms-son, and possibly the son of a werewolf, who features prominently in Egil's Saga

Skuggabaldur: a creature with a cat for a father and a fox for a mother, very dangerous to livestock and men

Skuld: one of the Nornir, whose special province is the future

Skyr: an Icelandic form of yogurt

Sólfar: a famous sculpture located in Reykjavik

Spádómur: Icelandic for "prophecy"

Sundhöllin: one of many public swimming halls frequented by Icelanders of all ages

Sunstone: a piece of glass formed magically from a shard of glacial ice to hold light

Surtur: lord of the fire giants of Muspellsheimur

Svartálfaheimur: one of the Nine Realms and home to the dökkálfar

Þór: the god of thunder and battles, known for his hammer Mjölnir

Týr: the god of war and justice

Urðarköttur: a ghoul-cat, created by burying the corpse of a cat in a graveyard for three years; can be trapped in its own reflection but can only be killed by silver buttons or bullets

Urður: one of the Nornir, whose special province is the past

Ùtburður: the ghost of an infant or child abandoned or exposed at birth

Valhöll: the hall in Ásgarður where honored warriors who die in battle reside until Ragnarök

Vanaheimur: one of the Nine Realms, home of the Vanir who warred with the Æsir and lost

Vanir: the secondary pantheon of Norse gods, including Freyja and her brother Freyr

Veðurfölnir: servant of Gammur

Verðandi: one of the Nornir, whose special province is the present

Vili and Vé: brothers of Óðinn

Yggdrasill: the World Tree, an immense ash tree and center of the cosmos that connects the Nine Realms

Ýmir: the first jötnar or frost giant, whose body was used by Óðinn and his brothers to form the cosmos

Yule Lads: the Jólasveinar, thirteen troll-sons of Grýla Trollmother who harass humans in the days leading up to Christmas. Among the Yule Lads are Skyrgámur, Ketkrókur, and Stekkjarstaur

Acknowledgments

I hope you enjoyed the conclusion of the story of Magnús and Altair (at least for now). If you liked FALCONGUARD, please consider leaving a review on Amazon, Goodreads, or any other social media. Ratings and reviews are incredibly helpful to independent authors like me.

Thank you to Erica Pike for helping me with Icelandic names and details. In particular, her meticulous research into the Latin school at Hólar that Galdra-Loftur attended in the seventeenth century was immensely helpful, though I admit to taking some liberties for story purposes. Please attribute any remaining errors with Icelandic names, idioms and locations to me or to the mischievous huldufólk.

Thanks as well to Andrew Hodges and Sara Kelly for their editorial assistance, to Kangsoon Park for my new author photo, and to Colin Abbott for his beautiful cover.

About the Author

Robert Winter is an award-winning romance novelist and recovering lawyer. When he turned 50, Robert left behind the (allegedly) glamorous world of international law firms and bankruptcy court to pursue his real passion. Now he lives in Montreal and on Cape Cod with his husband, studying French between trips to exotic locations.

Contact Robert at the following links:

Website: robertwinterauthor.com
Facebook: www.facebook.com/robert.winter.921230
Goodreads: www.goodreads.com/author/show/16068736.Robert_Winter
Bluesky: bsky.app/profile/rwinterauthor.bsky.social
Email: RobertWinterAuthor@comcast.net

ALSO BY ROBERT WINTER

Falconsaga Series

Falconsaga

Falconguard

Pride and Joy series

September

Asylum

Nights at Mata Hari series

Every Breath You Take

Lying Eyes

Holidays Suck! series

Vampire Claus

Fangsgiving

(Part 3 coming in 2025)

And writing as M.J. Edwards

The Escort's Tale